JORJA DUPONT OLIVA

Chasing Butterflies

IN THE UNSEEN UNIVERSE

Chasing Butterflies in the Unseen Universe (Book Three) by Jorja
DuPont-Oliva
Copyright © 2015 by Jorja DuPont-Oliva
Copy Edit by Nancy Quatrano
Cover design by Phat Puppy Art
Cover layout by Alexandra King
Interior layout and pagination by Michael Ray King
Chasing Butterflies in the Unseen Universe (Book Three) by Jorja
DuPont-Oliva
214p. ill. cm.
ISBN (softcover) 978-1-935795-42-1 (hardcover) 978-1-935795-41-4
Library of Congress Control Number: 2015917126

MRK Publishing
PO Box 353431
Palm Coast, FL 32135-3431
www.MichaelRayKingPublishing.com

Printed in the United States of America

Table of Contents

This story dedicated to

Gabrielle Smith

for being a star and making

the constellation complete.

~And also to~

My Mother and Father:

You will forever

shine in my

Universe.

The Chasing Butterflies in the Magical Garden Book Series was a Complete pleasure to read, You will get attached to Lizzy, Dee, and Ripley very quickly and follow a wonderful homespun tale about the ups and downs of true Friendships, Family, Life, Faith and Love.

Each Book is a build up to the next with its coming of age story line and hints of supernatural spirituality to delight and tingle your heart.

Author Jorja Du Pont Oliva's unique story is a breath of fresh air for your soul. Entering the third and final book, Chasing Butterflies in the Unseen Universe, She brings us to the future with reflections in the past, letting her creative imagination unfold so effortlessly you feel as though you have been transported along with the characters who have now become your friends.

You can tell in the wonderful writing this Author has a beautiful heart herself and knows how to weave a story that soon won't be forgotten~

These books are a fun heartwarming read, for young and old alike. Enjoy the magic~

Author Robin H. Soprano

ACKNOWLEDGEMENTS

To my father and mother, James and Linda DuPont, thank you for making me the person I am today.

To my husband and two son's thank you for your patience. **SMILE** my series is written!

To Gabrielle Smith and Rhonda Bracewell thank you for being my friends.

To Joanne Atkinson-Rest peacefully. Thank you for inspiring the bond between mother and daughter.

To Melissa Atkinson/Brock- Thank you for proof reading and being an inspiration to all daughters out there.

To Hope Brock-Thank you for picking up where your momma left off. Thank you too for the great ideas of how to organize my Chapters.

To Robin Soprano-Aiello- Thank you for getting my creative juices flowing and helping me come up with some great idea's. You inspire me! Your charisma is that of the truest of Authors!

To Luanne Laramore-Rest my friend. Thank you for encouraging me to write. Your battle with breast cancer showed me that life alone is a battle we can struggle through it or take it as you did-with grace. You inspired the Gracey story line and you have inspired me.

Michael Ray King Publishing
Nancy Quatrano/ On-target Words
Phat Puppy Art
Chris Balsam
Flagler Writers Forum
"Go write" classmates
The Beer House GANG
Countrytime Pub GANG
Photo by Jan
Janelle BarBour
Chasing Butterflies FAN CLUB
Angela Dossett
Lisa Stratford

To the rest of my family and friends, thank you for all your support and love!

"We are all stars in our precious universe, each one of us a separate star to shine our true gifted light. Invisible lines connect us together with no worry of distance or time, to make-up that perfect constellation."

-Jorja DuPont Oliva

"Bright star! Would I were steadfast as thou art-Not in lone splendour hung aloft the night. And watching with eternal lids apart, Like nature's patient, sleepless Eremite, The moving waters at their priestlike task Of pure ablution round earth's human shores..."

-John Keats

There is not one big cosmic meaning for all; there is only the meaning we each give to our life, an individual meaning, an individual plot, like an individual novel, a book for each person

~ Anais Nin quotes

We do not grow absolutely, chronologically. We grow sometimes in one dimension, and not in another; unevenly. We grow partially. We are relative. We are mature in one realm, childish in another. The past, present, and future mingle and pull us backward, forward, or fix us in the present. We are made up of layers, cells, constellations.

~ Anais Nin quotes

Prologue

Creatures of air and earth gathered in the garden. The sun fell into the earth for the evening as the moon peeked from the tall trees in the distance. The evening dew began to coat the ground.

"Why is it that we can see the stars and the moon only when the sun leaves us?" **asked the Rabbit.**

The butterfly, exhausted from flight, lands on top of the swan's back and exhales. *"It's time again for change."*

The swan nods her head. *"Soon the earth's shadow will cover the moon."*

"All we will be able to see in the darkness will be the stars," **the Dragonfly interrupted.**

"The stars we see here, in the garden, have passed," **vowed the eagle.**

The armadillo stomped in, nuzzling into the conversation. *"What do you mean the stars have passed? I see them!"*

"Stars we see here in the garden died out millions of light years ago." **The eagle spread his wings to explain.** *"Although we have been blessed enough to get to see their beauty here in the garden, they are no longer with us."*

"He is right." **The owl swooped down to make his way into their conversation.** *"As we glance to the stars, we are looking into the past. We are seeing the star's life as it once was."*

Sun and the earth slowly align with each other, as the earth's shadow graciously covers the moon. The creatures of air and earth process the stars' immortal existence.

"That's interesting, although the shadow of the earth has covered the moon, we know it is still there although it is unseen. Yet unlike the moon, the stars have passed on, but can still be seen." **The pigeon pondered the thought.**

More of the creatures of air and earth join the circle to watch the ending of the eclipse.

The Butterfly takes flight hovering over the circle and announces to the group, *"It is our responsibility to teach the humans, although the stars have passed on, they will still shine upon us."*

"And the generations after," **croaked the frog**.

The creatures of air and earth chattered with agreement, as the Earth's shadow uncovered to display the glow of the moon.

With each eclipse, appreciate the stars and learn from the moon. They will lead you, as they led her....

CHAPTER ONE

RIPLEY SEES REFLECTIONS

"Look at the stars, see their beauty. And in that beauty, see yourself."-Draya Mooney

2050

The year is 2050 and at eighty years old, in a world whispering, "nothing is the way it was" I, Ripley Smith Watson, stand closer to the end of my journey. *At least it feels like time dances by faster these days.*

My husband passed the year I turned seventy-four and at that point of my life, my journey *had* ended. The brightest of days had long since passed.

Questions of where I would go at the end of this journey called "life" are a constant these days. Would I have a legacy to leave behind for my family? My daughter Lindsey? My grandchildren? *Will I be just a memory for them? Did I teach them well enough? Was Dee right with her belief of transition? Was Lizzy right with the idea of heaven?*

I was never much of a believer in spiritualism or organized religion. Things were just as they were. I never questioned that. For years, I worked for my father at the hardware store and eventually the hardware store became my store. I saw life just as I did hardware. I called my belief system, *Hardware-ism.*

We need good tools to build a home, or a happy life, for that matter. Each tool has a job to do to help create each life and we build our own outcome. Might be a home, a child's treehouse or even a bridge to cross over a river.

I considered myself more of an atheist back in my younger days than I am now. Now, I teeter on the fence of belief; the fence I built with *my* tools.

I never truly believed in a higher being, but never completely doubted, either. To me, faith in that higher power was probably the one tool *everyone* wanted to have but never found: the tool that was perfectly fitted to their needs and got the job done.

That was always how I believed, and to me, Dee and Lizzy found their perfect tool.

I smile as I close the book I hold in my hand.

"Grammy, what-cha doin?" A tiny voice skips from down the sidewalk to the first step of my wooden porch and pauses.

"Oh honey, Grandma is just reading a book."

I stand from my rocking chair. The sound of the chair rocks back and forth on the old boards. My home stands as the oldest one in our town now. The Historical Society placed a "no touch" order on the property until I become content about developing.

The main road is lined with tall apartment buildings and high-rise offices surround my home. I imagine it probably looks like something similar to that old Star Wars movie. My home sits right smack in the middle of it all.

Because of all of my knowledge of hardware, I kept up the maintenance on my old house and that's the only reason my home still stands. Over the last ten years, the house has started falling apart though. Like the owner.

"What's a book?" The young voice moves up the wooden steps as her mother's footsteps follow behind.

"Hi, Mom."

I feel my daughter Lindsey's kiss grace my cheek and the small arms that match the petite voice, wrap around my leg. *My granddaughter Ashley.* Although I can't see well, I know that my granddaughter is the spitting image of Lindsey when she was that age.

"What's a book?" the small voice asks again.

I lean down, smiling at the foggy-faced little voice waiting by my feet.

"A book is filled with words on pages of paper. Not like those reading cards you have these days. Books have stories in them– magical stories that can take you to wonderful places in your imagination."

I gently rub my hand over top of the hardback book folded in my arm. I can feel my name engraved in the hard cover. I lean in for a kiss from the tiny voice.

"But Grammy you can't see very good, how can you read?" Ashley pecks a kiss and giggles.

"Well my dear, this book..." I rub my hand again over top of the hard cover book. "I've read so many times, I know it by heart." I whispered, "It's magical. I don't see the words... I *feel* them."

I get to my feet and turn towards the entrance of my home. Lindsey helps me find my way through the front door. As Ashley's footsteps follow, she asks, "Will you read it to me one day, Grammy?"

"I sure will, my dear," I answer.

***

Hours later, I sit at my small kitchen table, sipping a cup of homemade coffee. The aroma of the coffee rises slowly out of the steaming brew and helps me to get it to my mouth.

Mmm, nothing like a real cup of coffee. I sip and smile. Although the macular degeneration is slowly stealing my eyesight, I still know my way around my house and my kitchen. Thanks to the help of Lindsey and modern technology, I am still able to live out my days in my old home.

Lindsey installed automatic lighting and room temperature controls to the old house three years back. I even have a meal moderator that controls, cooks and serves a meal for me. They reminded me of the TV dinners I ate as a child.

My mother would tell me the TV dinners were like the meals the astronauts ate when in space. Anyway, I am sure to have a meal with no worry of trying to cook-just as the astronauts did. Of course, I still sneak and feel my way to a fresh cup of homemade brewed coffee when I can.

I sit with the hard cover book I'm so very fond of. I smile and lay my hand upon the top of it. It isn't just a book. As I confided in Ashley, the book *is* magical. With each page I turn, I regain my youth and my sight. Not only can I feel it but also I can see it, clearer and more vivid than the day I read the book for the first time.

I quickly sip down my coffee and stand. I need to get the evidence of my homemade coffee put away and cleaned up before Lindsey and little Ashley return from the Epic Mart–the fancy technology grocery store where Lindsey gets my meals for the week. It is the only grocery store to carry the meal moderator meals.

I shake my head. It's very easy, for even me, to cook these days. My opinion of how the world stands now? People are lazy. Content to have nothing to accomplish. They do nothing for themselves anymore, not even brewing a fresh cup of homemade coffee.

People aren't even sociable anymore. There's always some sort of crazy device that comes between them. Thank goodness, Lindsey and I believe in spending one on one time with loved ones. *I taught my daughter well enough about the important things in life.*

I dried my coffee cup and tucked it back in the cupboard.

"Mom? We're back," Lindsey's voice rang out. The sound of tiny feet dance along the wooden foyer floor behind Lindsey's voice.

"Grammy, I love how I hear everything in your house." Ashley skips over to me. "I can hear when I walk." She whispers, "Magical...Like your book."

Most houses built these days are assembled with sound proof everything: flooring, walls and ceilings. Mainly because people live in cramped spaces, with no desire to please one another. Respect for one another's presence has definitely become outdated.

"I picked you up some of that herb tea you asked about. They actually still make it." Lindsey pulls a box of tea bags from the metallic grocery bag. "It says you need to add hot water to it."

"Yes dear, that's how tea is made." I have to snicker. "I'm still capable of adding hot water." I smile as I take the box and feel my way to the cabinet. I place it on the bottom shelf so I'll know exactly where it will be, right next to my coffee cups.

"Mom you really should get rid of some of these old dishes. All your meals come with evaporating containers." I imagine Lindsey is looking into my cabinets. "All of these have to be washed after you eat. You don't need that extra work."

I place my hand on the cabinet door and close it. "I enjoy washing my dishes." I smile at my daughter's fuzzy face, which looks a little shocked, if I am seeing through the fuzz correctly.

"Grammy when can we read your book?" Ashley's voice calls from the table where the book sits patiently, unlike my sweet Ashley.

I make my way to the table and sit down beside my granddaughter. I pick up the book and open it to page one.

CHAPTER TWO

LIZZY FEELING DEPRESSIONS

"I have set before you life and death...Choose life so that you and your descendants may live."-Deuteronomy 30:19

2004

The year was 2004 and the year Lizzy turned thirty-four. BUCKETS anticipated Lizzy's arrival that rainy Monday morning. She turned the key until it clicked which allowed the door to open. Lizzy pulled the chain to turn on the pool table lights, one at a time. Each hanging light flickered a moment, just enough to warm itself to stay lit. The essence of stale smoke danced around the interior of BUCKETS.

Lizzy aligned and straightened the bar stools that sat as if someone had *just* stood from them. She moved to the end of the bar where she hung her purse on the hooks designed just for that purpose.

She exhaled. She did not feel quite herself these days. She placed her hand over top of her slightly swollen tummy and rubbed gently. She could feel the muscles stretching further than the first go round.

Three years had passed since the miscarriage but her fear of losing another child remained. *Incompetent cervix the doctor called it.*

"Incompetent," Lizzy was not. Of course, the one thing in the world she had wanted more than anything would be the one thing that she *was* incompetent at. Lucky for her, her doctor offered a procedure called a cervical cerclage, where they sewed the cervix closed until the delivery day of the baby.

Although it was costly, she and Joe made the decision to have it done. *With fingers crossed and prayers that this go round, nothing serious would happen.*

She would not ever be ready to accept the fact that she was not supposed to have children. Dee always told her, *maybe, it just isn't your time,* or *maybe, it isn't your fate.* This time, Lizzy felt that *she* was going to make it her fate. Although Dee, Lynn and even Ripley all offered to surrogate Lizzy's child–and she appreciated the offers– but that made her feel even more *incompetent.*

Lizzy's feelings caused friction in her marriage. In all reality, it caused friction in *all* of her relationships. She had always blamed her hormones when things where not right, so what made this time any different. Pregnancy always caused hormones to fluctuate, right?

"Hey, Liz," a voice echoed through BUCKETS.

She realized Dee was calling to her from the front door.

"Need anything from the store? I need to run over and pick up some stuff to pack in Henry's lunch tomorrow. He says he hates the preschool's food and refuses to try it."

"No...I don't know. Hold up let me check the kitchen." Lizzy disappeared into the kitchen for a moment then returned. "BUCKETS is stocked up pretty good but I could use some saltines. I can't seem to shake the sour stomach feel." Lizzy rubbed the top portion of her belly just above the baby bump.

"Ginger tea." Dee stepped through the door to explain. "Ginger root and hot water make a great tea and helps with upset stomach. Safe for the baby, too."

"Hmmm. Really?" Lizzy cocked her head. "Okay some of that, too. I'll try anything today. I'm not even sure I can make it through a whole day without puking."

Due to the drop in business, Lizzy and Dee were working a lot more than they used to.

"Is Joe coming home this weekend?" Dee looked concerned for her friend.

"Nope. Next weekend." Lizzy frowned her way to the register never looking up at Dee. She set up the register. Whining about having to survive without Joe being around was ridiculous. God knows, Dee lived a lifetime alone.

Financially, Lizzy and Joe struggled. The whole town struggled. Due to the declining economy and the speed of growth the town had endured the last several years, construction had slowed horribly. Joe closed down his business and went to work for a large corporation that worked all over the state of Florida and occasionally other states.

Lizzy and Joe had taken out a second mortgage on their home to finance the procedure on her cervix and help pay some bills they had fallen behind on, which caused them to fall further in the hole. Then construction came to a complete halt. Jobs were becoming a thing of the past and so was "extra" money.

"Hey, maybe you can go to the fish festival with me and Henry this weekend?" Dee asked excitedly.

"I don't think I'll be able to stomach the smell." Lizzy smiled. She rested her hand on her stomach again. "I made a customer a tuna melt yesterday and it took everything I had to get it out to him without puking. Besides I really don't have the extra money."

"Well, how about we come over and give you a hand getting your grass cut?" Dee opened the front door preparing to make her exit.

"Gosh Dee, that would be great. It is getting really high." Lizzy smiled, put her hand to her lips and blew Dee a kiss, now realizing Dee only wanted to let her know she was there for her. "You *are* the greatest."

Dee slipped out the door with a wave of her hand while Lizzy watched the door gently close behind her.

Things were not always peachy for the young women. BUCKETS was holding its own, but money was getting tight. Some of the regulars, one by one, were losing their jobs. Big corporations were laying off people left and right. Not only was their town suffering but also, the whole nation suffered. They called it a recession. It was more of a depression, thought Lizzy.

The only thing BUCKETS had going for it was the fact that when people and places were depressed, people drank. Lizzy and Dee felt quite lucky BUCKETS' doors still opened daily. They weren't moving forward, but they were holding on.

It all seemed to have started after Lizzy found out she was pregnant the first go round. And then her miscarriage. Not long after that, Joe took her to New York to visit his family and meet his aunt that worked in the twin towers.

One month later the towers fell due to a terrorist attack on the U.S. Luckily, two weeks before the towers fell, Joe's aunt was let go from her job. *A blessing in misfortune.* Not only was Joe's aunt alive, but it also helped Lizzy get over the pain and grief over the miscarriage.

The nation was now going to war on terrorism. The idea of fighting to the death and destroying the homes of people weighed heavily on Lizzy's heart. Now she feared for her own country, her own family, and now the child she was insisting come into her chaotic world.

***

Dee returned with saltines and gingerroot in a grocery bag from the big corporate super market that had opened just down the road. She sighed.

"Would you believe I tried three supermarkets before I finally found the ginger root? I probably should try growing it in my garden. Would you believe they charged me five bucks for one little root?"

"Holy cow that's expensive! The saltines would have been just fine, Dee." Lizzy glanced at Dee as she wiped down the bar.

"You only need to shave a little off for one cup. How are you feeling anyway?"

"Moody." Lizzy rolled her eyes.

"Come on girl, can't be that bad." Dee pulled the saltines and the ginger root from the plastic grocery bag.

Lizzy strived daily to keep a positive outlook but she struggled. Hard times and fluctuating hormones were like a battle of two demons.

Lizzy read her Bible daily. She prayed at every moment possible. She started to notice how many of the stories written in the Bible were similar to the chaos of the world today. She also realized another fact: man had written the words she read.

"I'm trying Dee. I don't want to whine or cry but I'm okay one minute, then I want to scream bloody murder the next." Lizzy gritted her teeth. "I don't even like myself right now," She hissed.

Dee, wide eyed, said nothing. She walked over to Lizzy and wrapped her arms around her. "I'm here," she whispered.

"I know you are. I just hate feeling like this. I've lost hope, in everything. How did our parents survive all the chaos, the worries, and the not knowing what the future held for us?" Lizzy pushed Dee away; she needed to fight this battle on her own.

Lizzy's parents were the best parents in the world to her, and only since she had become an adult did she notice they were aging; they weren't invincible.

Due to the drop in the economy and the price of everything going up, her mother and father, now in the empty nest stage, decided to start simplifying. They sold their house at the beach and moved into a small home with fewer expenses and less maintenance. Not long after that, Lizzy's father retired, and now on a fixed income, started having health issues.

Simplifying their life and minds, Lizzy's mother would say. They even drew up a will. *Just in case,* her mother assured her. That worried Lizzy, too. *I will someday have to face losing my parents. I don't know if I can handle that and a chaotic world, too.*

She shook herself out of her thoughts. "By the way, thank you for the saltines and the ginger root. I'm sorry to be such a bitch. I miss Joe. I miss how things were. Every day I walk into this place, I'm scared we'll eventually have to close and then what will we do to make money?" Lizzy paced the bar looking for a spot to wipe, waving the bar rag like a surrender flag.

Lizzy could see Dee's concern on her face, as plain as the day that she'd had the miscarriage.

"I'm sorry, Dee; I told you I was moody," Lizzy huffed trying to explain her odd behavior.

Dee's face relaxed, then she wrapped her arms around Lizzy again and whispered, "I'm here."

Lizzy knew Dee was at a loss for words and had no answers. *I'm being selfish, with the poor me crap.* She cleared her throat and pasted on a smile.

"So let's plan for Saturday," Lizzy said, extracting herself from her friend's arms. "You and Henry come to my house. I'll make us some lunch and we'll picnic in the pasture." She grinned at Dee.

"Sounds great. Maybe you could help Henry go fishing in the pond while I get your lawn cut. He would love that."

Dee grabbed her car keys looking a little more comfortable about leaving Lizzy at the bar with only one customer who'd watched the whole ordeal unfold. Luckily, there sat Head Phone Harry. He had his headphones on his ears the whole time.

"See you later..." Dee made her way out the front door.

Lizzy watched through the front window as Dee pulled away in her truck.

CHAPTER THREE

DEE HEARING HIS WORDS

"The way we talk to our children becomes their inner voice."-Peggy O'Mara

2004

The roads shined, wet from the rain that had graced them that morning. *Cleansing.* Dee still thought about the conversation she had with Lizzy earlier.

Dee was not much for worrying about life because life was going to happen regardless. Today she was not worried about Lizzy, but definitely concerned. *Maybe it was just her hormones.*

Pregnancy for Dee was just a big blur. Having had the blood pressure problems and pre-eclampsia, she did not remember much of the hormone issue.

She cautiously pulled the red Ranger into the preschool parking lot. She sat for a moment staring at the playground of the preschool. The moist glow from the rain covered the swing set.

The memory of the women's clinic she had gone to, almost five years ago, returned. *I almost had an abortion. I would have never felt this love or appreciation of family if I had gone through with it.* Dee had no regrets on her decisions. She looked at it the same way she did with life in general. Whatever was going to happen was supposed to, so why fret on it?

Everything happens for a reason. The one thing she'd wished had played out different was the fact that Henry would never know his father. The same *curse* she experienced, she had passed on to her son. Little Henry was a product of a one-nighter during Bike Week almost five years ago. It was not a mistake, for sure. It was supposed to happen Dee believed. It was karma teaching her not to dwell on her misfortunes but to embrace them. Now she had passed the same on to poor Henry. *My gift. Hah!*

"Stop it Dee, think positive thoughts," she muttered under her breath as she opened the truck door and got out. She made her way to the door that displayed a giant A, B and C.

As she opened the door to the pre-school, a little voice yelled out, "Mommy!" Henry raced to his mother and latched onto her leg.

"Hey Henry. Did ya have fun?" Dee asked with a gracious glance at the pre-school teacher that the children called Ms. Cee Cee, which actually stood for Carline Clair, but Cee Cee was easier for the children to say.

A thought about Lizzy popped into her head again. Lizzy always wanted to teach kids. *Did my dreams interfere with Lizzy's fate? Maybe that is why she's so discontent at BUCKETS.* Dee shook the thought away.

Dee bent down again and whispered to Henry with a quick rub on his head, "Go get your back pack and lunch box, sweetie." She then straightened to greet Ms. Clair. "Did he behave?"

"Always," Ms. Clair said with a smile that quickly faded. "It is none of my business but I'm asking because I'm concerned. Henry asked me today what a 'father' or a 'dad' was. I wasn't sure how to respond."

Perhaps the look on Dee's face answered her next question because the young teacher followed with, "It's just... we were making Father's Day cards this week and I don't know how to have him do the assignment. Is there a grandpa he could do the card for, or..."

"Have him do one for Uncle Joe; he *will* be a father soon." Dee smiled but knew her fair-skinned face had just turned bright red.

"Ohh, okay. Uncle Joe it is." Ms. Clair shook her head and obviously felt just as embarrassed.

Henry returned with his backpack and a giant smile. *He is a happy child.* Guilt consumed her again but Henry's beautiful smile washed it away.

She nudged him toward the door. Dee turned and whispered to the teacher, "I'll take care of the father-dad issue. I've dreaded this day but I knew it was coming." Dee nodded and opened the door for Henry.

What? Now I'm a bad mother because there is no dad in my child's life? After buckling Henry into his seat, Dee glanced back at Ms. Clair, who gave a smile and a wave.

Positive thinking, Dee. She was just concerned. He does need to know.

***

Dee turned the TV to Henry's favorite channel and kneeled beside him. Henry sat Indian style on the floor pushing a fire truck back and forth on the carpet. Dee wanted so much to explain to him about his father.

This was exactly what my mother must have felt. Please mother, help me say the right things. She looked at his innocent eyes and saw a whole *world* of explaining to do, which scared her into changing her thought for a moment.

"Do you want a snack, Henry?"

"Pe butter and yelly." He smiled.

"Oh, Henry. You always have peanut butter and jelly. How about some cheese and crackers or some grapes?"

"Pe butter and yelly, Mommy." He rolled the fire truck in a few circles on the carpet, "Varoooooom!"

"Okay fine, do you want a glass of milk, too?" Dee stood and headed towards the kitchen.

Henry paused the fire truck due to the sound of cartoons stealing his attention. "Yes, peese."

He got "please" from Lizzy. She was always saying please and thank you to him, just as her mother had done with her as a child.

Dee had not really noticed but she too had started saying her pleases and thank yous more these days. Maybe it was important to teach certain things to help a child become a grateful adult. Dee knew she was not ideal mommy material but she was going to try to be the best that she was capable of.

Sure, she was going to make mistakes just as her father had. *Damn it, I need to just go explain the father thing to Henry. Keep it simple. When he gets older, he can ask more. When he is ready, I can tell more.*

She slapped the top piece of the bread onto the sandwich, grabbed a sippy cup from the cabinet and poured Henry some milk. She picked up the plate and walked it into the living room where Henry sat in a trance in front of the TV. She sat down on the floor beside him. Moments passed of mother and son staring into the TV set.

"You know Aunt Lizzy is going to be a mommy just like me. Uncle Joe is going to be a dad, a father. They are going to have a baby just like you," she finally blurted out.

"I not a baby. I a big boy." Dee got Henry's attention.

"You *are* a big boy, but you are *my* baby." Dee was not feeling like she explained it right. "I am your mommy and..."

"You not want share me," Henry butted in.

Dee suddenly realized her son was smarter than she was giving him credit for. "All babies have a mommy and a daddy."

"Not me." Henry took a bite of his peanut butter and jelly sandwich.

"Yes, you do have a daddy."

"I does?" Henry looked up at his mother.

"I didn't have my father in my life either as a little girl. I thought he didn't want to be my daddy, but I was wrong." Dee exhaled; boy did she feel like she was screwing up.

"Mommy never told your daddy about you, because I didn't want to share. Mommy was being bad."

"Dat's not berry nice, Mommy. You always make *me* share."

"You're right, and that's why I am telling you now." Dee, at that moment, panicked. *I have no clue where to find his father. I can't tell him it was one night and I never even got his name. Dear God, what have I done to this child?*

"Can I see him?" Henry asked the dreaded question.

"Well, first Mommy needs to find him and then we will see, okay?"

"I can make him a Fadder's Day card dis week. Ms. Cee Cee says we make dem cards for Fadder's Day."

Dee saw the excitement in his face and the fact that he would be just like the other kids. The feeling of being normal. It tugged heavily at her heart, because she had lived her childhood being *that girl* that was *different* from everyone.

"Yes, you should make him a card." Dee and Henry sat in silence as the TV danced in front of them.

CHAPTER FOUR

RIPLEY'S DAY OUT

"Friends are like stars, you can't always see them but you know they are there."-Unknown

Ripley 2050

I stood at the edge of my wooden porch listening for the sounds of Lindsey's hover car to make its way to my driveway. Today was one of my special outing days. Every Wednesday, my daughter would pick me up to go to the Brooksville Nursing Home. Not only did I enjoy my one on one time with Lindsey, I also enjoyed my visits to the nursing home.

I always remembered to bring my magical book. So every Wednesday, like clockwork, the sound of Lindsey's hover car would grace my driveway. The air brakes whispered her arrival. Anticipation gathered in my stomach as I clutched the book to my chest. *This is my life now. This is the way my life is going to be.* Even though I loved living alone, I also loved spending time with my family and my friend. Today was one of those days.

"Hi, Mom." Lindsey's voice waited at the top of the wooden porch steps. "Are you ready?"

"Yes, dear." I turned towards my daughter's voice and followed it.

"Watch your step." Lindsey held my hand to help me down the steps. "One step at a time Mom."

Lindsey guided me to the car, the doors opened as we approached. She helped me into the car. A safety harness wrapped me into the seat. "I sure miss having a good old fashion seat belt to strap me in." I muttered. "These harnesses are suffocating."

"The harnesses are so much safer, especially in the hover cars. Hover cars can flip at the turn of a dime," Lindsey explained as the safety harness wrapped her into the seat, too.

"Mother, nothing is like it was. Things change, and they grow. Unfortunately, it is inevitable. Keeping up with it all is the real challenge." Lindsey glanced at me; I could feel her glare of frustration with me as she backed out of my driveway.

I just sat clutching the book, facing straight ahead, with a blank stare in my eyes. *I do not have to agree with her.*

***

After a wonderful lunch at the cafe with Lindsey and the robot server. I was ready for my visit to the nursing home. Lindsey pulled the hover car into the wrap-around driveway of Brooksville. The car door opened due to the signal the air brakes gave them.

"Hello, Mrs. Watson," a voice sang as the gentle hand it belonged to touched my shoulder. The safety harness unwrapped me from the seat. The voice grabbed for my hand, "We've been expecting you."

I knew that voice well and I could tell the voice had red hair through the fuzzy of my sight. *It's that sweet Kathy girl.*

"It's Nurse Kathy, Mom," Lindsey announced to me from the driver's seat.

"I know who it is, dear." I shooed my hand at my daughter and I patted Nurse Kathy's hand, which held mine.

"I'll be back at four o'clock to pick you up. Okay?" Lindsey yelled as I joined the nurse.

"I'm not going anywhere, unless I'm with *you, so* I guess the response has to be okay," I announced to the sound of the hover car. Which by the way was probably hard to hear by the average seeing person.

"We have Ms. Deidra waiting for you by her favorite window." Nurse Kathy guided me into the building.

"You can call her Dee. She *likes* to be called Dee." I smiled at the fuzzy redhead's face as the automatic doors closed behind us.

"By the way, we had another episode last night," Nurse Kathy whispered. "We found her in the kitchen yelling her name again. Almost like she was looking for her."

"Oh dear, thank God she was found. She could have harmed herself." I clutched the book even tighter to my chest.

I loved my one on one time with Dee, and I always remembered to bring the book along on my visits. It seemed the book was the only thing capable of bringing Dee back, even if it was only for a moment. That was why I believed the book to be magical.

After Lizzy's death, it seemed Dee had died too, well not physically. Dee's physical body remained in perfect health but her mind had died-or left. Although the doctors said Dee's mind would never return. I was not ready to accept that to be true.

"She's over here by the picture window that faces Brooksville's Garden." Nurse Kathy led me over to where Dee was sitting.

"Are there butterflies out there today?" I asked unable to see for myself. "What about the roses? Are they blooming?"

"Yes, Mrs. Watson. The garden is beautiful today," Nurse Kathy assured me.

"Great, today will be a perfect day for her." I sat on the chair beside my friend and opened the book.

CHAPTER FIVE

LIZZY'S EMPTY HOUSE

"Take heart, daughter; your faith has made you well."-Matthew 9:22

2004

Lizzy pulled into the long dirt driveway to her country home. She only lived ten minutes from town but now being alone most of the time it seemed to be hours from BUCKETS. She once loved to leave work and come home.

Today she was not so sure. She stopped at the mailbox at the end of her driveway to grab the mail. She quickly glanced through each envelope and noticed it was nothing but bills. Seemed these days as soon as a dollar or two was placed in her hand, someone wanted it and then some.

Joe called every evening to assure her that hard times were only a small hurdle for them and in time, they would pass. Lizzy had a hard time believing him. He stood as the positive one these days. Despite the overtime hours he would work just to have extra time at home with her, he remained positive. That is probably what bothered her the most. It seemed the harder they worked the more money every bill collector wanted. The mortgage was falling behind. As soon as they would get the mortgage paid the next month was due again. Sure, things happened like this constantly but they had always prevailed. This period seemed to have no light at the end of the tunnel. Just one long, dark, lonely tunnel. Lizzy turned off the ignition to the Jeep. Yep, she was still driving that old thing.

The new car idea Joe had a few years back happened but only for a year. They had financed a family car for Lizzy to drive and then everything started falling apart. They returned the car to the dealership exactly one year to the day they had bought it. So still having the Jeep was a blessing. Joe fixed it up some and gave it a fresh coat of paint. He sold the vintage Trans-Am to a collector for some good money but had to turn around and get a reliable truck to use to travel for his new job.

Lizzy got out of the Jeep and made her way up the redwood deck to the front door. Sprawled lazily across the entrance was Tank. A giant dog–Presa Canario to be exact. Tank was a rare breed, new to the states. They originated from the Canary Islands. Joe's dream dog. Joe wanted to get this particular breed as soon as they had property big enough for a dog that size. When the opportunity arrived, Joe jumped at the chance. Joe wanted to breed the specific mastiff breed, and do the dog show thing, maybe make a few bucks at it too.

Tank had just turned three, the age their miscarried baby would have been. Tank did not show a lot of enthusiasm unless someone or something he did not know tried to enter their property. That was the only reason Lizzy was not scared to stay in her home alone. Well, in addition to the fact she had a shotgun she knew how to use, thanks to her daddy. Times were hard for everyone. Home invasions talk all over the local news channels, helped fuel some fear.

Tank loved Lizzy more than he did Joe and Lizzy knew it. Probably because Lizzy babied him so much as a puppy. She was his mommy.

"Hey, Tanky, baby." Lizzy knelt and rubbed Tank's massive head. Tank huffed out a grisly growl and two taps from his tail but otherwise didn't move. "Are you hungry buddy?"

Tank stood from the door as fast as a dog his size could move. His tail moved much faster now with his giant front paws stomping with anticipation. His head was level with Lizzy's baby bump; he sniffed twice, as if to make sure the baby was still there.

"Let's get you some dinner." Lizzy stuck the key into the door and unlocked it then pushed her way into the silence of the empty house and Tank followed happily behind her.

"Where's my Bella girl?" Lizzy called out into the silence. The click clack of dog toenails danced on the hardwood floor towards the foyer where Tank and she stood. A smaller, female version of Tank met them. Lizzy knelt and gave a quick rub to Bella's head. Tails waged with excitement of Lizzy's presence. They both licked her face as she tried to stand upright, which made her smile a bit.

"Wanna go outside pretty girl?" Lizzy opened the door a little wider and Bella launched out the door.

Tank followed her to the yard sniffing each step Bella made. Lizzy watched from the door as they danced, excited to see each other. Bella ran and Tank chased, as if Bella knew he would follow her anywhere. They were the only thing keeping Lizzy sane and her loneliness from taking over completely.

He does not seem so lazy now. Bella and food would liven Tank up a bit. Bella did not stop to notice either. Seemed Bella and Lizzy had something in common; inability to breed and inability to see how much their mates even cared.

Bella and I are two of a kind. Lizzy closed the thought away as she closed the front door and the dimness of the house grabbed her attention.

She clicked on the floor lamp that stood beside the couch. The light showed nothing but the way around an empty house. She wanted to yell out that she was home, but to who? A shadow of Joe's that might have stayed behind from his last visit home? *Not with miserable me.* At least that was how it seemed. She felt disconnected from everything, including the man she loved and adored.

Lizzy glanced down at her Bible, which rested on the coffee table in front of the couch. She moved toward it, picked it up and plopped on to the couch. She opened the Bible and a paper fluttered out of it, which she did not find odd, considering she constantly stuck thank you notes and poems she had written in it.

This one was different; she had written a poem one day at work for her first-born child before she had ever become pregnant. Back when having a child was just a thought. It read:

Precious child, I love you dear.

You are only a thought, I can see so clear.

I have dreamed of you from the time I was small.

Wanting to catch you from every fall.

Lizzy smiled at that moment and then the smile faded. She turned the piece of paper over noticing it was from a flyer she had made for BUCKET's Bike Week BBQ, five years ago.

A phone number with the name "Alo" danced in red ink over top of it. *Whose phone number is this? It is my hand writing...Lizzy* thought hard for a moment then tucked it back into her Bible and stood.

She made her way to the kitchen. She opened the pantry door, scooped out two giant scoops of dog food and walked to the matching stainless steel bowls. She dumped both scoops into the bowls. She picked up the two water bowls and made her way to the sink.

The poem popped into her head again as she filled the bowls, and again the phone number. *Alo, who is Alo?* Having pregnancy brain was almost as bad as no brain at all. Everything was a fog. Even the sign of being happy again seemed to dismay her.

Once Tank and Bella were fed and watered, she opened the cabinet to see what she would feed herself. Lizzy's love of cooking had even subsided. *Can of chicken noodle soup and saltines.*

Once she sat down and ate, she resumed some of her energy. *Let's get the rest of the flock fed.* Lizzy slid on her boots and stood. She glanced at Bella and Tank snuggled together beneath her feet and smiled, but it only lasted a moment.

Lizzy made her way to the barn. She scooped out a bucket of chicken feed and worked her way to the coop.

"Hello, Ladies."

Chickens gathered excitedly around Lizzy's boots. She sprinkled the layer feed on the ground and dumped the rest into the chicken feeder. In the coop, she checked each box for eggs and gently added each one into the bucket so they did not break.

Back at the barn, she scooped up a large bucket of cracked corn to take to Wilber, the pig Joe wanted to get. *We can raise it for its meat,* he had persuaded her. When the time came for Wilber to go to the butcher, Joe couldn't let him go. He loved Wilber too much. Lizzy knew naming the pig Wilber was not the greatest of ideas but she also understood Joe's attachment to him.

"Howdy, Wilbur, Momma's brought you some supper." Lizzy dumped the corn into the metal trough. If her belly grew to much more she was going to need help keeping up with all of the animals. *Then I'll be even more incompetent.* Her laugh was harsh, but she could not seem to shake her gloom.

Once her chores were done, she returned to the house. It was time for Joe to be calling, so she waited to take her nightly shower. Oh how she missed him....

At that moment, the phone rang. Lizzy rushed to the phone and answered.

"Hello?" For a moment she smiled then she felt her smile fade. She felt her shoulders sag.

"No, I promise I'll take care of it as soon as possible. Yes, as soon as possible. Thank you. Again, I'm sorry. You'll be the first on my list." Lizzy hung the phone up.

It rang again. Shaking with frustration, she snarled into the phone, "I said I'd take care of it!"

"Hey, Baby. Take care of what?" Joe asked.

"Damn bill collectors. I can't take this anymore, Joe!" Lizzy lashed out.

He was silent.

"Joe, I'm sorry... are you there?" Lizzy whispered through the receiver.

"I'm here, honey."

"I miss you," she whimpered.

"I miss you, too. Baby, go outside onto the porch." Lizzy followed his directions holding the phone in her tight grasp.

"Look up... What do you see?" he asked.

"Stars, the moon," Lizzy whispered.

"I am seeing exactly the same thing. Pick a star," Joe said.

"The brightest one to the left of the moon." Lizzy made her choice staring into the sky.

"Perfect choice. Let us look at it together... Now, let's make a wish," he whispered through the phone.

For that moment, Lizzy didn't feel so all alone staring up at the stars. "I made a wish," she said.

"Me, too," a voice said from behind her.

Lizzy spun around quickly and there stood Joe with his cell phone in his hand.

***

Lizzy tucked herself underneath Joe's arm as they relaxed on the couch watching the TV. Joe had the opposite hand resting on Lizzy's tummy, which held his baby.

"I still can't believe you're here," Lizzy mentioned again for the last of many times, realizing her wish had come true.

"I am. Glad I am, too." Joe kissed Lizzy's forehead. "Got to go back in couple days. So let's make the most of our time."

"Really?" Lizzy sat up and looked at him.

"I got a raise, Lizzy, and we start a new job this week. So they let us off a few days early, because the next job is going to be a doozy. A lot of overtime." Joe smiled staring at the TV. "Maybe it will help us get some bills caught up."

Lizzy was disappointed he had to go back so soon, but was thankful more money would be coming in. She eased her way back underneath his arm.

Tank and Bella snuggled in the middle of the living room floor. Each time Joe or Lizzy spoke, they raised their heads to listen. They too had become accustom to a silent house.

"I can't wait to get you upstairs," Lizzy whispered in Joe's ear.

Joe just smiled, his attention riveted to the television. Which bothered Lizzy. Was something wrong? He didn't seem to care about making love with her, even though he'd been gone for weeks. *Is it because of the weight I put on? Why doesn't he seem excited to be with me?*

Lizzy was putting on weight and losing her self-confidence at the same time.

Lizzy nuzzled closer to Joe. *At least he is home. Something about his smell always comforts me.* When he was gone, Lizzy wore Joe's undershirts to bed–she believe it helped her sleep better. At least when he left again, his scent seemed to stay behind. Silence lingered between them but the TV sounds echoed through the house. It was the most noise in the house in weeks.

"Do you want me to make you something to eat?" Lizzy knew Joe loved her food. And that would be a sure way to have him get excited about being home.

"No, no, I stopped on the way home and grabbed some food. I would love some of your pancakes in the morning." He sent her a smile.

"Ok...Pancakes it is." Lizzy nuzzled.

Hours later, she woke on the couch, alone. Had she only dreamed he was home? Tank and Bella laid in the exact spot. Lizzy sat up on the couch. All the lights were off and TV was off. No sign of Joe. She made her way up the dark staircase to their room.

Once she entered the room, she turned on the bathroom light. The light trailed into the bedroom and made a spotlight onto the bed where Joe's body laid clutching her pillow.

Without me. Lizzy wondered why he did not wake her to come to bed. She turned off the light and gently crawled into the bed. Joe's arm let go of the pillow and wrapped around Lizzy's body and he pulled her to him. Then he kissed the back of her head. He fell quickly back to sleep.

Doesn't he want me? It's been weeks.

***

Lizzy woke extra early to spend time with Joe, before having to run off and open BUCKETS. Joe was peacefully sleeping. The sun was just an inch from breaking the horizon. The trails of light were anticipating a day of sunshine. She brushed her teeth quietly and then her hair, added a hint of make up to not look as if she obviously was trying to look pretty. She left on her silky nighty and headed downstairs to prepare pancakes. Since her exhaustion had ruined their time together last night, today would be a new start.

She started a pot of coffee and pulled out a pan to cook the pancakes in. She glanced down at her belly that seemed to expand more each day. She smiled and gently rubbed it. She grabbed another pan to cook the sausage patties and slapped six of them into the pan. In a bowl, she started the pancake batter.

"Oh, can't forget to add some vanilla extract," Lizzy babbled and put two teaspoons of extract into the batter. That was her mother's secret to delicious pancakes.

It sure smelled good. The sizzling of the sausage released an aroma of breakfast that must have made its way upstairs, because Lizzy could hear Joe bumping around above the kitchen.

"He is up and moving around now," Lizzy mentioned to the patties as she turned each one. The pancake had bubbled just enough to flip.

"Perfectly golden." She lifted her coffee and sipped. "Oh, so good." Lizzy limited her coffee intake these days due to advice from her doctor. She savored that one cup a day.

"Smells wonderful in here!" Joe stood in the doorway with a grin on his face.

Disappointment consumed Lizzy again. "You're already dressed…" Lizzy said. She wasn't even quite sure if she was asking or telling.

"Yeah, wanted to get a jump on the day. Maybe see if I can get that lawn mower working and get some of the pasture cut."

Lizzy dropped the spatula onto the counter and turned to Joe. "I thought maybe you would want to be intimate with *me* this morning, not the lawn mower." Her frustration was apparent. If she was not being noticed before, she sure was being noticed now. She slapped the

pancakes onto the plate, then the sausage, and handed it to him
without even a glance at his face.

"Lizzy, we need to talk..."

He steadily held his plate with a look of dread as if he wanted to
tell her something that might upset her.

Lizzy felt the sheer blanket of panic cover her body. *Dear God,
could he be wanting a divorce? His car was what he used to turn to
when his relationships weren't working.* Lizzy remembered that time
of their lives very well. She wanted to be a friend and help him
through his rocky relationship, but she couldn't–she'd already fallen
in love with him.

*He is trying to avoid me. Oh, my God could there be another
woman?* In that one minute of stark silence, several scenarios played
out in her head. Her eyes filled with tears preparing to fall as he made
his way to the table to sit.

"Come, sit." He nudged his head at the empty chair she usually sat
in.

CHAPTER SIX

DEE SEES THE GIFT

"I wish I could show you when you are lonely...or in darkness the astonishing light of your own being."-Hafez

2004

Dee stood at the screen door sipping her herbal tea. She watched Henry talking to the butterflies that were fluttering about in the garden. *Could he have the gift?*

At that same moment, she noticed a daisy had grown in the garden. Henry bent down and spoke to the butterfly that had landed on the daisy.

"Hey dare Yoey… want to pay in the daisy field?"

Dee was not sure what she had heard but what she did know was that Henry was talking to someone or something in her garden.

Could it be? She had never planted daisies in the garden, and ever since Henry was born, her intuitiveness seemed to have almost diminished.

Henry again bent down and spoke to the butterfly as if he knew it well. *Could that butterfly represent Joseph? Should I mention this to Lizzy? Lizzy and Joe's first born was to be named Joseph.*

The past few years the garden still flourished but it just did not seem as magical as it once was. The doctors had told Lizzy the baby she had miscarried was a boy. He probably would not have been healthy even if he had made it full term. His development did not appear to be the normal for a 5-month fetus. That was what they had originally blamed the miscarriage on before they noticed her cervix was thin. The deciding factor of the miscarriage was an incompetent cervix.

That too is probably weighing heavily on Lizzy as well. She's worried about having an unhealthy child.

Today while Henry played about in the garden, the plants and insects seemed to be even more alive. The colors of each flower more vivid. The whole garden followed his every movement, as if he *was* the gardens nourishment. Henry's essence was something of an enhancement for the plants and the insects. Dee watched in amazement. *His essence is much stronger than mine ever was.*

The ringing of the phone startled Dee. As she made her way to the phone, she made one last glance at Henry in the garden to grasp again, how magical it was. She answered the phone.

"Hello?" Her breath caught in her chest. Lizzy was beside herself.

"What's gotten you so upset?" she asked. Then she listened.

"Sure, I'll be there as soon as I can. What's going on?" Dee was very concerned.

"He's home? Lizzy calm down. I'll see you in about twenty minutes. I promise." Dee hung up the phone.

"Henry come inside! Mommy needs to go to BUCKETS to see Aunt Lizzy a minute. Come wash your face and hands."

She dropped down on the couch and slipped her shoes on as Henry entered the screen door. "Sweetie take that shirt off too and put a clean one on."

"O tay." Henry peeled the shirt he wore off and threw it to the floor. Dee stood and followed behind him picking the shirt up on the way to his room.

As they got out to the truck, Dee hoisted Henry up into his car seat and buckled him in. She kissed his forehead. "I love you."

"Loves you too, Mommy." He smiled.

They arrived at BUCKETS at the same moment Lizzy pulled into the parking place out front. She looked as though her world had fallen on top of her. *What could Joe have possibly said to her?*

On the phone all Lizzy had said to Dee was that she needed to talk. Joe had told her how he was really feeling and she needed to figure it out. She was awfully upset and Dee knew it was important. She turned off the ignition, opened the truck door and glanced back at Henry who had fallen asleep on the ride.

"Are you ok?" Dee asked as red-eyed Lizzy stepped out of the Jeep.

"Joe doesn't want to have sex with me." Lizzy wiped her nose on a tissue she had obviously used several times. "He's scared. He's afraid he might damage the cervix. He doesn't want us to risk losing this baby."

"Oh Lizzy, he's being honest with you. That's sweet," Dee said. That obviously was not what Lizzy wanted to hear, by the look on her face.

"Is he?" Lizzy's tone matched her expression. "Or is it an excuse?"

"Come on, Lizzy. Joe loves you, girl. He's absolutely crazy about you!" Dee wrapped her arms around Lizzy who broke down crying.

"He does. I know he does. I just have all these crazy thoughts going on in my head. I feel so unattractive. I want to show him how much I miss and love him, but it's like he's avoiding me. I haven't been the most pleasant person… *That* I do know." Lizzy sniffled again.

"You've had a world of problems you have been trying to carry on your shoulders. So has he. Just breathe. Things are going to get better. They always do." Dee rubbed Lizzy's back for a moment then clutched her shoulders to look her in the eyes. Dee glanced down at Lizzy's belly and noticed it seemed to have doubled in size since yesterday. "Holy cow that baby is growing!"

"I feel huge... I guess my belly has really grown a lot since Joe last saw me. Maybe the size of my belly is what scared him, not the fact I put on weight. Seeing my tummy bigger probably struck a reality nerve." Lizzy's mouth turned up a bit almost as if a smile was about to appear.

"Are you going to be okay to work?" Dee cocked her head and waited for an answer.

"I'm better now. I just needed my *rational* brain to work my thoughts out. That's you! You always help me figure out my thoughts. Thanks." Lizzy wiped her nose and inhaled a cleansing breath. She fished her keys from her purse and shook them with a fake smile.

With Lizzy's back to her as she unlocked the door of BUCKETS, Dee yelled, "I'll come in early tonight so you can have time with Joe. You know, you *can* show him you love him without endangering the baby."

Lizzy stopped in her tracks. She turned with a real smile on her face. "You're right!" A hint of a giggle followed. "That would be great if you can get here early. He only has a couple days before he has to go back."

"See you at four o'clock, then." Dee hopped in her truck and turned to peek at Henry who was still peacefully sleeping.

***

Dee pulled the truck into the driveway of her home and glanced at Henry who was still sound asleep in his car seat. *He looks so much like his father.*

Henry had a toasty warm tan tone to his complexion, unlike Dee's fair skin. His hair was also much darker than her hair was. More of a brown than her cinnamon red color although a hint of red highlighted his tips which glowed out in the sun light. He sported her green eyes though.

Dee smiled. *He is my everything... Am I ready to share him with his father if I do find him?* Dee shook the thought away and unbuckled her seat belt, swung her legs out of the truck and stood.

Across the street, she noticed Johnny pacing, talking on the cell phone in front of the shop. Dee waved to him and he returned the gesture, and then continued pacing.

Hmmm... That is so not Johnny. He always yells out something. I wonder what seriousness has his wheels turning?

She worked her way to the passenger side of the truck and opened the door. She quietly unbuckled Henry from his car seat careful not to wake him. She cradled him in her arms, gently tip toeing towards the house.

After she laid him on the couch, she stood above him staring. *How blessed I am to have him. I need to remember as much as I can about Henry's father, just in case I'm unable to find him.* Dee went into the kitchen sat down at the table grabbed a note pad and started jotting down anything she was able to remember.

Approximately five-year's ago-1999? Henry was born in 2000.

BUCKETS first annual bike week BBQ(CHECK WITH LIZZY ON THIS)

Black silky hair and olive complexion-Hispanic? No accent. Italian? No, very straight hair.

Dee stopped a moment, tapping the pen on her cheek desperately trying to remember. She started to write more.

Tribal tattoos ran up his arm. Indian maybe? (SKETCH tattoo)

Days Inn by Interstate 95. Could he have stayed another night there? (CHECK OUT)

He had a bare chest. Not a lot of hair. Tribal tattoos on chest. Native American look. (LOOK INTO THIS.)

Dee smiled. She actually felt like she was getting somewhere, and was enjoying the memory of that night. *He was a beautiful man. Even today, I have no regret. Well, I guess now I regret not getting his name. He had such a perfect body...Maybe Henry will share his father with me?*

"Mommy, I's hungry." Henry entered the kitchen rubbing his eyes.

Dee almost jumped out of her chair. "Oh...you're awake." She stood, setting the pen on the table next to the note pad.

"Do you want Mommy to make you a grilled cheese sandwich with some soup?" She was slowly learning to cook. Grilled cheese was one of the first cooked foods Lizzy had taught her to prepare. *Kids love grilled cheese,* Lizzy had told Dee.

"No Mommy, penutter yelly," Henry yawned.

"Honey you need to eat something other than peanut butter and jelly sandwiches." Dee put her hands on her hip. "How about some carrots with dip? Or..." Dee walked to the fridge and opened it. "Some fruit? Peaches, applesauce?"

"Appsauce and penutter yelly." Henry smiled.

How can I resist that smile? Oh, he has his father's smile. Dee rushed to her notes and jotted that down:

His smile was beautiful. Large, attractive smile...The best part. Very soft spoken.

"Okay, kiddo. Applesauce and peanut butter and jelly it is." She laid the pen on the table and then rubbed the top of his head on her way to the cabinet. Out came the large jar of peanut butter that she placed on the counter next to the breadbox. Then she scurried to the fridge for the jelly and applesauce. Henry watched with his sleepy eyes and hair all a mess. Dee scooped a big scoop of applesauce from the jar, plopped it into a small bowl. She put a spoon in it and walked it to the table.

"Here honey, eat this while I make your sandwich."

Dee thought, at least he would get some applesauce down before he got his sandwich. She smiled as she watched him scoop up the first bite.

After Henry finished his lunch, Dee admired him as he went to his room and dug through his toy box. He came out with a plastic flute type whistle. He marched throughout the house and whistled as loud as the flute could scream.

"Henry! Outside now." Dee commanded as she washed up the dishes from lunch. Henry skipped his way to the screen door. He exited with the slam of the screen door as the sound of the whistle followed. *My little pied piper.* Dee smiled at the thought. *Dishes done. I'll have my tea now and join Henry in the garden.*

Moments later Dee joined her piper in the garden where he was skipping about among the flowers and plants. Dee sat on the swing absorbing the beautiful end of spring sunshine.

Summer solstice approached and screamed out its arrival with authority. Dee sipped her tea watching her little pied piper. She thought back to the story she remembered her mother telling her.

A stranger came to town and lured all the rats from the town with the song from his flute. Dee smiled at the thought. She remembered as a child picturing the pied piper as her father, coming home to lure her family from the town.

Dee bolted upright on the swing. *Oh my God! That's it!* Dee jumped up from the swing and rushed her way into the house. She went over to the pen and paper and jotted down one more memory:

Tattoo on shoulder-hunch back with whistle or flute. (SYMBOL ALMOST GEOMETRICAL-SHAPED) Like rock carvings-ancient Native American work.(CHECK ON) Art work maybe?

Dee tapped the pen on the table three times. Suddenly more of the tattoo artwork popped into her head. She started to scratch more thoughts on the note pad.

Horns, serpent snake-like image. A star, more symbolic. Not mainstream tattoos.

Dee remembered how mesmerized by his artwork she was. Okay the perfect body also had her attention. Dee huffed out a small laugh. *The memory of his body made me completely forget about the artwork.* Dee smiled. She was happy with all she had recalled from that night. A re-connection of a sort. A familiar feeling.

I need to go check on Henry. Dee glanced out into the garden where Henry blew his whistle that now seemed to be more of an enchanting song of hope. She watched him for moments, and then realized the butterflies were following him. The bees too, followed. The flowers swayed to the movement of the plastic whistle. *Like a snake charmer. Hmmm...*

CHAPTER SEVEN

RIPLEY'S WISH

"There wouldn't be a sky full of stars if we were all meant to wish on the same one."-Frances Clark

2050

"I, Ripley Smith, take you Allen James Watson to be my wedded husband to have and to hold from this day forward." Ripley's nervous hands shook while his large masculine hands held them tightly as if never to let go. His big crystal blue eyes pierced forever into her soul. Lizzy and Dee stood beside Ripley as she recited her vows to Allen.

"I, Allen James Watson take you Ripley Smith to be my wedded wife to have and to hold from this day forward." Allen vowed. The "this day forward" was part Dee's idea, because "death do us part" made Ripley cringe at the thought of ever losing Allen.

Allen graciously bent down to Lindsey, whose dress matched her mother's. "I, Allen James Watson take you, Lindsey, as my daughter to have, to spoil rotten, and love to the best of my ability." Sweet

Lindsey smiled up at the tall handsome cowboy. Allen tipped his hat at the little girl as he turned to the preacher.

"You may kiss the bride," Pastor Dan announced as a slight breeze blew throughout the pasture, to the guests seated on hay bales behind the couple as they kissed. The three turned towards the guest and blew kisses.

Lindsey opened her basket and released twenty butterflies out into the wide-open space. The Watson twins walked two horses towards the threesome. Allen lifted Lindsey onto a horse then helped Ripley mount. Then he mounted his horse and they waved to their guests. The three of them rode out of the pasture and into the sunset.

***

The memory of my wedding day plays out in my head like an old western movie. Today is a day that everything seems to make sense.

Lizzy made sure that on my wedding day I had a preacher do the ceremony and not just a justice of peace as I'd originally planned.

Dee was excited about her idea to release butterflies at the end, which Lindsey too had been eagerly awaiting.

I have lost the majority of my sight but the imagery in my head is still as vivid as the day the event played out, thanks to the magical book.

Many memories I thought were lost now surfaced again. Just recently, I realized how much I need these memories in my life. *The memories of lost loved ones remind me what is important. Memories are all I have left.*

I stand from my worn sofa, which too has many memories that still linger around it, just waiting to be remembered. I smile at that sofa, thinking back to one particular memory.

The first time Allen and I made love was on *that* same sofa. That is the only reason I keep it around. No matter how many times Lindsey tries to talk me into getting a new one, I refuse the idea. Sure, the sofa is an antique but so am I. Antiques and I belong together. I think back again to the past…

***

"We have the house to ourselves. Lindsey is with her father," Ripley whispered in Allen's ear as she kissed his neck and removed his cowboy hat. She unbuttoned each button of his shirt, exposing his chest and tight abs. He was a thin man but had a large masculine frame. She pulled the shirt over his broad shoulders, kissing every exposed piece of his chest. She ran her fingers through a small patch of blonde hair in the center of his chest. Two shades darker than the hair on his head. They fell onto the couch...

Ripley laughed. "Your boots." She stood eagerly pulling one boot at a time grinning from ear to ear. She unbuttoned his nicely fitted Wranglers and then straddled him.

"Are you sure? Are you sure this is what you want? I can wait..." He moaned as she kissed her way up each inch of his body.

"I have waited too long for this," she mumbled through each seductive kiss. She dragged her bottom lip upward to his lips, leaving a moist trail the length of his body.

"God, Rip... I can't take much more," he drawled as she took each part of him, absorbing him, taking him to become part of her.

***

~ 48 ~

I nod to that old sofa today and to the memory. I may not be able to see how worn that sofa is but I know how attached I am to the memory. *Oh the memories that still sit upon it.* I suppose that is why people hold on to old things. It is not so much the item they keep as what lingers along with them. That old sofa still makes me smile.

I feel my way to the kitchen and move my hand along the counter towards the cabinet, which holds my coffee mugs and the herbal tea bags Lindsey bought for me. I retrieve the cup and the tea bag. *Where could I have put that teapot?*

Patting my way around on the shelf, I suddenly find it, feeling like a little girl who has just discovered a new doll. I fill the pot and then made my way to my antique stove and turn it on.

Yep, another thing I insist on keeping. I hold my hands just above the glass top burner. I feel for the heat, then place the teapot on it. When the whistle sounds its shrilling hiss, I carefully pour the hot water into my cup.

I carefully feel my way to the small kitchen table with tea in hand. I sit down my cup and reach out to pull the book in front of me. I open the book and lift my tea to my mouth. I take a sip. *Magical.*

***

I have never been much for having wishes such as, becoming a bar owner or getting married, as my friends always had. I never set goals of what I wanted to accomplish or experience. My goals were mapped out for me the day I was born.

Hardware: my grandfather was the first Smith to open the hardware store, then my father inherited it, and then me. I was the only child, so it was *my plan, my fate.*

Until now, that is. Now I know what *God's plan* is, as Lizzy would say. I am what I am, a Smith, and never looked at my life as lacking anything.

Somehow, today's day and time needs my old ideas. Maybe at some point I might have invested some interest in things that were not in my comfort zone. Maybe jump out of that plane like Dee wanted to do, or write that best-selling novel Lizzy wished for, or even climb Mount Everest, like Allen had written on his bucket list. Something that would have defined me as a person besides hardware.

Some of us are just happy staying where we are, I guess. Today I am happy they dragged me along on those wishes. Experience is the key to living life.

It's Sunday morning and I planned to attend church today. Yep, me at church. Another thing losing favor in "today's world." There are very few branches of religions and churches these days.

I was never much of a "churchy" kind of woman. After Allen passed, I needed "something" to make it through the rest of my so-called life and Lizzy suggested I come along with her on Sundays. Lizzy explained how much it had helped her deal with Joe's death. So every Sunday Lizzy came by and picked me up and we attended church together. Some days Dee would join us. Until Lizzy passed, that is. I blink the thought away.

Today Lindsey is sending Jeffery over to drive me to church. It's the only thing left to consider believing in. I still need something to hold onto, don't I?

Jeffery is my grandson, Lindsey's oldest. Lindsey had Jeffery at a suitable age and the year he turned eighteen was the year Lindsey found out she was pregnant again. Lindsey was in her fifties at the time and I was terrified for her. Back in my day and time, having a child at that age was not even heard of and the survival rate of that child was very slim. But Lindsey had our Ashley safe and sound, thanks to modern medical technology. I shake my head. That's another thing....

Hell, many women these days don't even have to carry their children. They grow them in pods so the pregnancy won't damage their bodies. Almost as if God or fate is being taken out of the equation of life. *No magic left in today's world.* The "damage" to my body was what I embraced most about my pregnancy with Lindsey. And she felt that way about Ashley, too.

"Gram!" A young masculine voice interrupts my thoughts. Followed by footsteps on my hardwood floors, the voice continues, "Are you ready?"

I sip down the last of my coffee as Jeffery enters my small kitchen. He's a tall boy and looks a lot like my father looks in my childhood memories. Lucky enough for me, I'd gotten to see that in Jeffery before my sight had started degenerating. Jeffery was also lucky enough to have spent some years with Allen before he passed, unlike little Ashley.

Life is made up of what we remember, wish for and most of all, the scars that have healed.

"Yes dear," I answer counting from memory how many steps to the sink. I rinse out my coffee mug and leave it to sit in the sink. A devilish giggle rumbles my belly as I think back to the hard times I gave Dee and Lizzy about leaving the dishes in the sink and running off.

Jeffery links my arm into his. "May I escort you?"

I pat his arm, proud to be leaving a well-mannered descendant for the world to appreciate.

After Allen's death, I flooded myself with wonder. I'd only retired from the hardware store a few years before he died. I still carry that secret regret, taking care of that store and not spending more time with him before he passed.

Lindsey never showed much interest in the hardware business and I never forced it on her, either. A year before I retired I sold it off to Dee's son, Henry. He was always building and working on projects that required tools.

The store always intrigued him. Even as a young boy, he would come along on visits with his mother. He'd aimlessly walk around, mesmerized by all of the tools and hardware the store offered. Dee always said it was his calling.

"Gram? Are you feeling all right?"

I realize I have been daydreaming again. Oh well. I'm old. Daydreaming is a good thing. I smile at him.

"Oh, dear, I'm fine. Just thinking back is all." I gaze ahead. "You have grown to be a fine young man, Jeffery. One a grandmother like me is very proud of."

I tilt my head upward to face my grandson. I have fuzzed vision but maybe he can see in my eyes how proud I am.

I know that at least one of my wishes has come true.

CHAPTER EIGHT

LIZZY IS HUGE WITH HORMONES

"Now faith is the substance of things hoped for, the evidence of things not seen."-Hebrews 11:1

2004

Where the hell is Dee? Lizzy thought. Even though she realized she was over reacting a bit about Joe's concern for her and the baby, she also realized, she could not even see her feet anymore. *Could there possibly be anything less attractive than that?* One minute she felt like laughing, the next she battled tears.

"How did it go today? Feeling better?" Dee's voice snapped Lizzy from her thoughts. "I'm not as early as I had hoped and I'm sorry. Ripley will come by to get Henry after she closes up the hardware store."

Henry stood next to Dee smiling up at Lizzy. "Hi Aunt Izzy."

Why wouldn't she ask me? "Ripley is going to watch him for you? I would have taken him with me if you didn't have a sitter."

Dee walked to the register to see if she needed to change out any small bills. "You and Joe need time alone, Lizzy. Ripley was excited to get to hang out with him."

Lizzy, now content with Dee's reasoning kneeled down and hugged the little boy. "You are growing up too fast." She rubbed his head as she stood up.

"Aunt Izzy, you belly is fat," Henry announced.

Lizzy and Dee were wide-eyed in shock. They both started to laugh. "There is a baby in here." Lizzy rubbed her belly.

"Dhere's more dhan dat," Henry added and they laughed again so much that it caught the attention of the only two customers seated at the end of the bar.

The front door opened and in walked Ripley and Lindsey. "We are here," Ripley announced and made her way to Henry. "Henry, want to go to McDonalds with us? After that you can come to my house and play with Lindsey." She put out her hand for him to latch onto. Only a few years back their small town had opened a fast food restaurant by the interstate, so going there was a treat for any one under the age of fifteen.

"Can I sleep over too?" He asked.

"Yes, you can have my bed," Lindsey added.

"The princess room?" he asked with a giant grin on his face.

"Yep," Lindsey said.

"You are getting huge," Ripley said to Lizzy as she reached her hand out to touch Lizzy's belly. "Are you sure you aren't having twins?"

"Henry seems to think there is more than one baby," Dee said as she joined the group. She bent down to kiss Henry.

"You behave for Aunt Ripley and Ms. Lindsey. Brush your teeth before you go to bed. I'll come get you first thing in the morning," Dee said to him with a smile.

Now looking down at her stomach Lizzy said, "We're scheduled for an appointment for a sonogram at my next doctor's visit." She looked up and smiled. "Maybe Henry's right!"

They all laughed. "Okay, kiddo, you ready?" Ripley asked Henry. He nodded. She turned to her daughter.

"Lindsey, go get the car seat from Dee's truck and load it in to the van." She turned to the little boy. "Got your bag?" she asked.

"Yep!" He lifted the overnight bag that was as big as he was. Ripley took it from him.

"Wow, how long you plan on staying with me?" She smiled down at him on their way out the door.

"Just tonight," he said looking up as he held her hand. He glanced over his shoulder as they exited the door. "Bye, Mommy!"

"Bye, sweetie. Be good," Dee yelled. She turned to Lizzy. "Go home, spend some time with Joe. He'll only be home another day, right?"

"Yes, you're right," Lizzy replied not feeling so sensitive about Dee not asking her to watch Henry. She grabbed her purse and headed for the door then turn back to Dee. "Thank you."

"Welcome," Dee replied with a nod.

***

Lizzy pulled the Jeep into the dirt driveway of their home. Joe's truck sat patiently in the drive. A sense of comfort came over her. As she turned the ignition off, she noticed Joe was nowhere in sight. A wonderful scent of garlic and herbs permeated from the house. Tank and Bella met Lizzy as she opened the Jeep door.

"Hey, guys!" She stepped out of the Jeep–their tails waged profusely. "Momma's home. Smells like your daddy's cooking in my kitchen." She patted both of their heads and headed towards the front door.

As she opened the door, the living room appeared dim. She worked her way to the dining room and noticed the small table wore a red satin tablecloth. Two candle tapers flickered in the middle of the table. Her finest china waited in front of both chairs. Her grandmother's crystal wine glasses twinkled next to a bucket filled with ice where a bottle of sparkling grape juice was nestled in it.

Lizzy smiled. It had been at least two years since the two of them had been out on a romantic dinner date. The funds were never available. With Joe constantly traveling, sitting down for even an average meal was a rare experience anymore. *What has he done?*

"Hello, Beautiful," Joe's voice called from the kitchen.

"It looks so pretty." Lizzy admired the well-set table. She turned to Joe.

He stood in the doorway of the kitchen holding a box wrapped in the most beautiful gold paper.

"Open it." He pushed the box towards her. Joe, dressed in his best Sunday clothes, which were hiding underneath Lizzy's cooking apron, pushed the box again. "It's for you."

"What did you do?" Lizzy asked knowing damn well that they could not afford any extra purchases these days.

"I got you a dress. I hope it fits." He smiled, still pushing the box towards her. "A beautiful woman needs a beautiful dress."

Lizzy knew she would not be able to fit into any of her dresses in the closet, at least not for a few months more. She smiled and took the box and began to open it.

"I had to drive thirty miles north of here to find a maternity store. They only had a few dresses to choose from. Now this one, looked *almost* as beautiful as you." Joe excitedly followed her as she opened the lid of the box.

Lizzy pulled the dress from the box admiring how beautiful it appeared.

"Wow!" She stared at the dress then placed up to her body. It sure looked like it was going to fit.

"Now go get dressed. We have a date tonight." Joe winked at Lizzy and made his way back into the kitchen.

Lizzy stood for a moment. Suddenly a tickle of excitement consumed her. *Butterflies.* She rushed up the stairs into the bedroom. Joe had placed rose petals all over the top of their bed. Small scented candles flickered in every corner of the room. Soft music played off in the distance.

Lizzy washed up as fast as she could, and then slid the beautiful dress over top of her swollen belly. She shot a small spritz of perfume on her neck, then went to the closet and slipped on her favorite heels. She returned to the bathroom and added some flavored lip-gloss. *Only a touch.* Lizzy inhaled a cleansing breath. She glanced at the bed and straightened her beautiful dress over top of her belly.

Lizzy sauntered her way down the staircase, more because she was balancing the heel-belly ratio. It sure gave her an elegant flow to her entrance. The corners of her mouth turned up. She realized how silly she had been. Always struggling to be perfect and unhappy with life when obstacles stepped in the way. *I'm going to go with the flow. No expectations. No worry of perfection.*

Lizzy smiled at Joe as she entered the dining room. "You look absolutely stunning." He reached for her hand then swung her into his masculine arms.

Lizzy laughed. "I still can't believe you did this for me."

"I did it for *us,* my dear," he whispered along her throat and stopped with a gentle kiss.

"It smells delish. What did you cook?" Lizzy turned facing the elegantly set table, as Joe cuddled her from behind still nibbling the base of her neck.

"Penne pasta with a marinara sauce." He kissed her neck again. "Chicken cutlets," he whispered into the nape of her neck. "Antipasto." He said on an exhale, seemingly lost in her scent.

When Lizzy turned back into him, their lips met. In the moment of pure sensuality, Lizzy's breath escaped. "It's going to get cold."

Joe stopped and they stood for a moment with their foreheads holding each other in place. "I love you." He sighed, staring into her sparkling eyes. He kissed her forehead.

At that moment, she realized her feeling of loss were not about making love with Joe. She missed Joe's attention and the feeling of being attractive. Special. Knowing he still desired her.

He does want me.

CHAPTER NINE

DEE IS CURIOUS

"The important thing is not to stop questioning. Curiosity has its own reason for existing."-Albert Einstein

2004

"Hey, sweetie, what are you drawing?" Dee kissed the top of Henry's head.

She had arrived at Ripley's house early enough for Ripley to head off to open the hardware store. Dee offered to put Lindsey on to the bus.

"Hi, Ms. Dee." Lindsey slung her backpack over her shoulder and stood in the kitchen doorway.

Dee turned towards the doorway. "Hey girlie, you ready?"

"Yep. My mom wanted me to feed the cat before we left."

"Did you do it yet?" Dee asked.

"Nooo." Lindsey smiled.

"Get to it then. The bus comes in ten minutes."

Dee turned back to see the picture Henry was working on. The picture had two stick figures playing in a field. A field of daisies.

"Are those sun flowers?" Dee asked only because they were as tall as the stick figures.

"Daisies, Mommy, like we have in the garden," Henry answered.

"Is that me and you?" Dee's curiosity drew her closer to the picture.

"Nope. Dats me and my friend," Henry explained.

"What's your friend's name?" she asked noticing it did look like two small boys.

"Yoey," he said. Dee's eyes widened.

"Done." Lindsey's voice snapped Dee from her surprise.

"Okay." She glanced once more at the picture and rubbed Henry's back. "Come on Henry, let's get Lindsey on the bus." Dee stared at the picture as Henry moved his chair and stood.

He has The Gift.

***

Long after getting Lindsey on to the bus and Henry off to day care, Dee made her way to BUCKETS. Today was going to be hectic. Thoughts of Henry's drawing kept her mind racing.

I need to focus. I lived with the gift my whole life and I turned out fine. His gift did not scare her, it was the thought that someday she would need to explain it. Or would she?

"Howdy, stranger." A male southern voice caught her attention.

"Well, Allen Watson, how the hell have you been?" Dee smiled making her way to the tall figure standing at the end of the bar. "Good god, I haven't seen you since high school? What were they feeding you in the military? You're almost two foot taller these days."

"I guess my growing spurt came after we graduated." He laughed. "My momma said the same thing happened to her brother Ottis." He glanced around BUCKETS. "You and another girl we went to school with own this place?" he asked looking around BUCKETS.

"Sure do. Lizzy—we were all in Mrs. Miller's homeroom. Blonde curly hair. I wasn't friends with her back then."

"Yeah, she bought the old Lacey's place. Next door to my daddy's land," he confirmed.

"That's her." Dee smiled. "How ya been?"

"Good. It's nice to be back home. You look good, Dee. Happy even." He nodded as though the idea pleased him.

"I am." The corners of her mouth turned up. *I guess I would look happier than the last time he saw me.* Dee realized the last memory of Allen she had was at her mother's funeral. He was one of the few people that really made her feel normal or not so weird. "Are you married? Got any kids?"

"Nope. And Nope." Allen shrugged, then smiled. "Seems I'm one of the last ones left."

"No, a few of us are still single. Hell, some are working on second marriages already. Hey, wanna beer?" she asked as she threw a coaster on the bar top.

"Sure. I thought maybe you and Ripley owned this place. I remember she moved in with you not long after your momma died."

"Yeah, she did." Dee smirked. She could tell he still had an eye for Ol'Ripley. "She is running her daddy's hardware store. She has a beautiful daughter named Lindsey."

Dee watched as disappointment covered his face. "As a matter of fact, I put her on the bus this morning for Ripley." His expression now looked as if questions circled in his head. "She never married."

"Really?" He sipped the ice-cold beer Dee placed in front of him. "She was such a pretty girl."

"Guess she hasn't found the right guy." Dee made her way down the bar and into the kitchen. She poked her head out. "Excuse me a minute, Allen. I need to get the soup of the day warming. Lunch crowd will be coming in soon."

"Yeah, no problem. It *is* great to be home." He took another sip of his beer with a sheepish grin on his face.

He wants Ripley, for sure! Dee thought as she proceeded to pull out the goulash Lizzy had made yesterday. She dumped it into a pot and turned the burner on low. As she turned around, Gracey startled her by standing in the doorway of the kitchen.

"Can we talk?" Gracey asked. Her face was white as a sheet.

"Sure." Dee grabbed a paper towel from the dispenser and wiped her hands. "Come out here..." Dee went to the bar and pulled a stool out. "Sit."

Gracey let out a long breath as she set down. She whispered, "I just found out that I have breast cancer."

Dee's heart stopped mid-beat. *Oh dear God.* "Are you sure?"

"Yes." Gracey fumbled with her fingers. "You're the first person I've told. Harry doesn't even know yet. The results just came in this morning." A tear rolled down her cheek.

"Oh God, Gracey." Dee wrapped her arms around her. She suddenly had an urge to speak in her motherly tone. "It will be all right, you hear me?" Dee cuddled Gracey's head into her arms and tears flowed.

"I'll catch you later."

Allen's voice caught Dee's attention. She looked up to see him getting to his feet, and waved. The look on his face was concern. Dee knew he understood that they needed BUCKETS to themselves.

CHAPTER TEN

RIPLEY WANTS TO LIVE

"When I die choose a star and name it after me, that you may know I have not abandoned or forgotten you."-David Ignatou, "For My Daughter"

2050

"I can't believe you just up and left me here," I say aloud with my head pointed toward his gravestone.

I kneel and place the bundle of flowers in the planter that sat affixed to the stone. "Damn you...," I huffed, then calmed myself. I gently rubbed my hands over top of the lettering carved into the stone. I could feel what it read:

Allen James Watson

"Cowboy"

1971–2044

Beloved Father and Husband

For a few moments, I rub my hand on the stone and I listen to the sounds of the graveyard. *Pure silence. Peaceful silence.* The wind rustles the trees contained within the block wall of the cemetery. The only *real* old-fashioned cemetery left.

Today, most people are cremated, and put into storage bins they called Resting Ashes. A big, high-tech "die" rise that stands at the edge of town.

The cemetery is the perfect place for Allen to rest because he adored the outdoors. I jump as something crawls across my hand. I gently feel it to see what it might be.

A caterpillar, which in today's day and time is odd. I slightly pinch it; just enough to pick it up and put it on the flowers I brought.

"Now, eat little fellah, so you too can become a beautiful butterfly."

At that very moment, Dee and her Butterfly obsession comes into my mind. Dee believes when people die they become butterflies or plants. I realize just then, why I am still alive.

Lindsey stayed back in the hover car while I visited Allen's grave. She respects my moments with him. Although Allen was not Lindsey's biological father, she still loved him as a father and because he was always there for us.

Lindsey was only nine years old when she had met Allen. He was never able to have children of his own so he took to Lindsey as if she was his. He spoiled her rotten. I suspected Lindsey had a hard time when he passed, just as I had, but she has always avoided the subject.

Everyone handles death in a different way. Only three years after Allen died, we had to face the death of Lizzy. Doctors said it was a heart attack. I think it was more of a broken heart. Joe was her everything.

I figure Lindsey now fears the thought of losing me before too long. When Lizzy died, Dee's dementia progressed to the point that Henry could no longer care for her and put her in the old folk's home.

He visited her often but would always tell me that she'd gone the day Lizzy died. At times, I knew he was right, but at some moments Dee was back home with me and we were in the magical garden enjoying each other's company. *Oh how I miss my life, my youth, and all of those I loved.*

"Mom... Are you ready?" Lindsey's voice travels around my shoulder and to my ear. I stand and don't say a word. I do not really want to leave him.

"Mom?" Lindsey touches my shoulder. I quickly wipe the tear that's fallen, then turn to my daughter.

"Please, dear," I start, "When I am gone... Remember me."

"Oh, Mom."

Lindsey grabs me by my shoulders and latches a hold of my frail body. She hugs me with every ounce of herself that she has. She looks me in the eyes–I could feel the stare.

"You are part of me...I will always remember you. You will live on in me. You will live on in my children. You will always live on." She gently rubs my back. I know for Lindsey to say that, it must have taken a lot, because Lindsey was never good with dealing with death.

"Mom...Look at me." I look toward my daughter's foggy face. "If there was, or is, one thing you wish you would have done...what would it be?" she asks.

A tear slowly works its way out of my eye. "I wish I would have lived."

The words just came out. I'm not sure what I meant.

***

I stand at my kitchen sink washing my dishes from the quick breakfast I had before leaving with Lindsey to go to the cemetery. I celebrate when I wash dishes.

It's a joyful event for me. I celebrate each spoon I wash, each plate and each coffee cup. I celebrate the fact that I am able to eat and drink and the dishes are proof.

It is my strange joyful event, no matter how simple it sounds. I think back to the conversation with my daughter at Allen's gravesite.

What did I actually mean by "I wanted to live"? I don't remember resenting that, but maybe I have. I never actually did things that I thought of doing, at least for myself. I did for everyone else with no hesitation but never for myself. No path to choose, no decisions to make, just a road set for me to travel. My thoughts traveled again to the past.

***

"I want to be with you when Halley's Comet passes the earth again." Ripley shot a quick smile at Allen as she thought back at the two of them at thirteen years old.

Standing out in the cow pasture with him as she towered over him, they watched the sky, waiting to see Halley's Comet pass the earth for the first time in their lifetime.

They might not have actually gotten to see Halley's Comet pass overhead, but they knew for certain what was happening between them.

"That was the same year the space shuttle Challenger exploded," Ripley said to him.

"You know, I had such a crush on you back then." Allen smiled staring up at the night sky. "I think I still do," he mumbled.

They laid on the top of the hood of his truck watching a meteor shower sparkle throughout the darkened sky.

"I had a little crush on you, too," Ripley said with a laugh. "I stood a foot taller than you, so I ignored my feelings." She laughed again. "I didn't want to have to bend down to kiss you." She giggled glaring at the star lit sky.

"I also worried about people making fun of us...the tall girl with the short guy."

The darkness surrounded each beautiful star that graced the sky that night, like glitter on a black velvet cloth.

She shook her head in disbelief. "Then you show back up here...taller than your average guy! You were meant for me."

"Well, little darlin', I want to be with you too. That is, when Halley's Comet passes the earth again. It's every seventy five years though, so that would be...2061. Let's make a date now." His smile grew. "But that means you would have to marry me," he whispered and turned facing Ripley. He cleared his throat. "Rip, would you marry me?"

***

I smile at the imagery in my head as I dry my hands on the towel, but then I remember there is not going to be another chance to see Halley's Comet with Allen. He always had a good way of walking through one idea to get to another. That was something I loved him for.

That thought makes me realize something about myself. I always wanted to travel to places I had never been....

***

"I want go to Louisiana–to the bayou," Ripley admitted to Dee as she relaxed on the swing in Dee's garden.

Lizzy walked up on the conversation holding a tray with three glass of sweet iced tea. The summer sun's rays scorched with enough heat to melt the mascara from your eyelashes.

"I've always had some kind of connection with the bayou," Dee countered.

"I've always wanted to write a novel," Lizzy added as she plopped on the swing next to Ripley.

Dee stood from pulling weeds and wiped the dirt from her hands and the sweat that rolled down her forehead.

"Now me...I want to jump out of a plane. Yes a perfectly good plane." Dee grinned. The three of them laughed, and sipped their sweet iced tea.

"I think Ripley has the most realistic dream." Dee toasted to the air. "We could..."

"We should do it. We should go to New Orleans. Just the three of us. It would be fun." Lizzy suggested.

***

It was a place Allen and I had always *talked* about seeing, but never followed through on. The girls and I never did either.

That's what I'm going to do. I'll take a trip to New Orleans and go to the bayou.

"We should do it. We should go to New Orleans. Just the three of us. It would be fun," I hear Lizzy's voice say again in my mind.

CHAPTER ELEVEN

LIZZY EMERGES

"For I reckon that the sufferings of this present time are not worthy to be compared with the glory which shall be revealed in us."-Romans 8:18

2004

Lizzy's eyes fluttered and slowly opened. She moved the blonde curl that had fallen in her face to make eye contact with the digital clock. *Five AM.* Joe busily packed his clean clothes into the suitcase.

"I thought you weren't leaving until seven."

"I wanted to get this done and loaded," he said as he crouched beside the bed. "So I can get back in bed and cuddle some more with you." He grinned.

Lizzy smiled and reached out to caress his cheek with her fingertips. They had cuddled naked all night. It was orgasmic, reverent and very erotic. Who would have thought no sex could be so fulfilling? By the look on Joe's face, it was just what he had needed, too.

"Hey, you mentioned Dee coming over and helping mow some of the grass one weekend. Do you think she could finish what I didn't get done?" he asked as he returned to packing.

"I can do it. It isn't that much," Lizzy answered.

"I know you could... I would just feel better if she did it and not you." He stood from the bed.

He's so worried about me. Lizzy smiled. "You're right. All the bouncing probably isn't a good idea." She shrugged and winked at him. "I'm sure she won't mind."

Joe quickly finished packing and took the suitcase out to his truck. Lizzy listened as he scurried back up the stairs. He grinned from ear to ear as he undressed.

Lizzy lazily watched him eagerly jump into bed next to *her*. They explored each other's bodies with their hands, as if memorizing every nook and cranny. They inhaled each other's pheromones only to savor one another's essence.

"I'm sooo gonna miss you," Joe growled as he nibbled Lizzy's neck.

"You better." She giggled trying not to fight the tickling sensation.

***

Hours after Joe said his goodbyes, Lizzy hesitated going down stairs to the empty house. As she finally emerged from her closed chrysalis state, she entered the living room. Tank and Bella's tails tapped the hard wood floor to greet her. "I know... I'm going to miss him, too," she said to them. They both wore sad expressions, as if they knew exactly what she meant.

She sat down on the couch and picked up a pad and paper. It was actually her journal. She wrote in her journal a lot. Most of her journaling was at times of depression. It always seemed to clarify why she had to go through hard times.

What is the reason for my loneliness? Why do Joe and I have to go through this? What is it we are supposed to learn? At that very moment, she started writing. An epiphany of a sort. Words flowed from her pen. She was a writing goddess. In addition, it, felt, *good.*

After writing everything she had in her head onto the paper, she took a breath, like a whale in the deep blue sea, coming up for air. Tank and Bella glanced up as if Lizzy glowed. Both dogs whined with excitement–they too felt the energy.

"I'm going to write a book," she announced. "I've always said it, so why the hell not?"

She closed the journal shut and laid it on the end table. She glanced at her Bible, which sat next to her journal. She picked it up and the paper with the poem and the phone number fell from it again. *Who is Alo?*

"Only one way to find out..." Lizzy got to her feet and headed to the phone.

***

Lizzy jumped in her Jeep, almost afraid to let her secret out to Dee, knowing damn good and well Dee would be opposed to the idea. She cranked the Jeep to go find Dee and talk it out.

She felt the baby kick and kick again. "Wow." For that single moment, she was hypnotized, waiting for another, almost addicted already to the feeling of life inside her body.

My first pregnancy, the baby barely moved... I've got to talk to Dee.

Shortly, she arrived at BUCKETS. She rolled the Jeep into the parking lot and exhaled. *I just have to be straight up with her. Honest.*

Lizzy got out of the Jeep and headed for the front door.

"Hey, Miss Lizzy," a voice called from a tall fellow just leaving BUCKETS.

"Allen Watson! It has been years," she said.

"I heard you bought the old Lacy place."

"We did." She rubbed her belly and smiled up at him.

"You aren't still with Lee, are ya?"

"Heavens no, I married a guy that wasn't from around here." Lizzy blushed.

"You and Dee own this place… I would have never pictured you in this type of business." Allen lifted his hat and scratched his head. "Well, I got to get going. Hope I get to see you again." He nodded, replaced his hat and walked on.

Lizzy opened BUCKETS' front door. At the end of the bar sat Dee and Gracey. *This doesn't look good.* Lizzy cautiously walked towards them. She noticed they were both crying.

"Oh dear, what's happened?" Lizzy asked, almost afraid to hear the answer.

Dee looked at Gracey. "Do you want me to tell her?"

Gracey nodded,

"Gracey was diagnosed this morning with..."Dee cleared her throat and whispered. "Breast cancer."

"Oh, God...." Lizzy wrapped her arms around them both. At that very moment, she knew she had to write that book.

The secret she was in such a hurry to share with Dee was forgotten somewhere between the conversation with Allen Watson and Gracey's upsetting news.

CHAPTER TWELVE

DEE'S WISH

"The true mystery of the world is the visible, not the invisible."-
Oscar Wilde

2004

That evening Dee sat at her kitchen table thinking about Gracey.
She was not big on worrying over problems: to her, things never
happened the way the world wanted them to; they happened the way
fate wanted them to.

But tonight she worried. She knew what Gracey had told her was
not good. Dee's mother had died from cancer. Gracey too, had lost
her own mother from cancer only just a few years back.

Gracey's a fighter. I know she'll be okay. Dee could hear Henry's
sweet giggle coming from the living room. She stood to see what
amused him. She glanced at him where he sat cross-legged on the
living room floor in front of the TV. She moved closer to the
doorway.

"What-cha watchin'?" she asked, then took a quick glance at the TV and noticed it was not on.

"What's so funny?" she asked softly. Henry giggled again holding his hand cupped in front of him.

"Just playing. Yoey says he wants me to take care of his sisters when they come."

"Sisters?" Dee asked moving closer to Henry. "How old is your friend?"

"My age. He is a little bit smaller." Henry raises one hand just a hair below his own head, with the other hand grasping tight to something.

"You can see him?" Dee asked.

"Yep, but he is really fuzzy, Mommy." Henry smiled at Dee.

"Tell me more about... Yoey, is it?" Dee sat Indian style on the floor next to Henry.

"Yoey, not YOOey." Henry corrected.

"Joey?"

"Yes, Mommy. He's my friend. We play a lot in the garden. He can't leave the garden, though."

"How are you able to see him in here, then?" Dee asked.

Henry lifted his cupped hands, gently opened them and in his palm a small butterfly desperately fluttered; one of the wings looked damaged.

"Oh dear, we need to get him to the garden, Henry." Dee helped Henry to his feet while she explained the urgency.

"The Native American Indians believe that if you capture a butterfly and whisper your wish to it and then release the butterfly, it will carry your wish to the Great Spirit." Dee opened the door to the garden. "By setting the butterfly free, you are helping to restore the balance of nature and your wish will surely come true."

"But, Mommy..." Henry pleaded.

"No 'buts'," she said as she opened Henry's hands and released the butterfly out into the garden. "Did you make a wish?" She smiled at her son who was not looking very happy with her.

"I did..."

"Why the sad face, then?" she asked placing a finger underneath his chin to lift his face so she could look at him.

"Yoey wanted me to take him to Aunt Izzy's and Uncle Yoe's. Let him go... there by the lake. That was... *his* wish..."

"Oh honey..." Dee kneeled in front of him. "Maybe we can catch him again and take him this weekend. He needs to stay out here to survive..." She stopped when it dawned on her what was happening.

"He just wants to be with his mommy and daddy. Just like I do..." Henry explained.

The phone in the house rang and caught Dee's attention. "I'll be right back, Henry. You stay put."

The sun had fallen and the dusk sky was beginning to darken. Dee answered the phone.

"Hello?" She glanced out the screen door and into the garden at Henry. "What?" She turned away. "Are you sure it's Henry's father?" she whispered into the receiver.

"Well I'll be damned," she muttered when she hung up the phone. *Gotta be careful what you wish for, I guess....*

***

The night progressed slowly for Dee. After giving Henry his bath and milk and cookies before bed, she'd finally gotten him to sleep. The whole time, her phone conversation with Lizzy echoed in her head.

"Dee, he wants to see you," played over in her mind the most.

"I didn't mention Henry to him," took second place.

"I had no idea whose number it was. I just called and asked if he had ever been to our town. He is from Arizona. I asked if he had ever been to BUCKETS. He asked if my name was Deidra. He is coming here, Dee." Lizzy's worried babble played again in her head. *"I came to BUCKETS to tell you about the phone call, and then I somehow got caught up with Gracey and the breast cancer. Pregnancy brain I guess."* Lizzy had explained.

She knew her friend was upset; she could hear the tears in her voice. Dee paced the floor in her kitchen. *I'll get to know him first. No mention of Henry until I feel comfortable. Definitively comfortable before Henry gets to meet him. Dear God, is this what I want?*

Dee had been thinking about finding Henry's father for weeks now. *Alo–Lizzy said his name was Alo.* It would seem that fate was making it actually happen. She was scared shit-less. Now questions swarmed her head.

What if he is nothing like I remember? Oh... he was sexy, all right. What if he's angry with me? What if he doesn't accept Henry as his? Of course, one look at him and he'll know that's nonsense. Do we do a DNA test?

Dee plopped down in the chair at the kitchen table. "Dee, you sure make a mess of things," she sighed aloud. She was absolutely exhausted.

The Gracey worry; dealing with Henry and his gift; needing to get the butterfly caught and brought to Lizzy and Joe's house; now the thought of seeing Henry's father again. That *alone* was exhausting–exciting–but exhausting. Erotic–but exhausting. *Oh...he was sooo sexy.* Dee slowly drifted off to sleep still sitting in the chair.

***

Alone in the forest Dee attempts to walk, but with no legs, she in unable to move forward. She glances down at her feet that seemed attached to the ground. Roots! Her feet are roots–grounded to the earth.

She attempts to move her arms. Her arms are not arms but branches. The ground appears to be defrosting from a cold winter. The dampness of the earth dances in the shadows of the tree. Henry plays in the distance with a small boy. He is safe and carefree, Dee thought.

Although she cannot get to him, she feels content. She glances at her limb and on a small branch sits a butterfly. In the distance, Henry plays happily.

A large male shadowy figure steps out from behind a maple tree. For a moment, fear rustles her leaves. The butterfly takes flight and joins Henry and his friend. The shadowy figure doesn't appear to be as dark as it seemed at first.

Colors start appearing as the light moves above the treetops. He is just watching the children play. He means no harm, she thought or felt. The shadowy figure is a man. Is that Henry's father? He can't know about Henry yet. I'm not ready for that. She cautiously watches the figure. He never shows any sign of aggression. He looks more like he admires him.

Dee notices two more children join Henry and his friend. They are two little girls much smaller than Henry and his friend. They are wearing beautiful yellow Easter dresses and holding hands. Chocolate brown hair with Lizzy's beautiful curls. They are identical twins...

***

Dee woke sharply and sat up in the chair. "Twins! Lizzy is having twins," Dee said aloud. "Girls, twin girls."

Henry had said Joey wanted him to look after his sisters. Dee realized she had not lost her intuitiveness–she still had it. *I need to pay more attention to my dreams.* Although years had passed since she'd had any sort of epiphany, the gift was back.

As for Henry's father, he will be whatever he is supposed to be....

CHAPTER THIRTEEN

RIPLEY'S SECRET

"May the stars carry your sadness away. May the flowers fill your heart with beauty. May hope forever wipe away your tears. And above all, may silence make you strong."-Chief Dan George, **"Inside the Divine Pattern"**

2050

Today is the beginning–the beginning of *something*. I'm not quite sure yet what that something is but what I am sure of is that I am going to live.

I wait on my old wooden front porch just as I have done every Wednesday, listening for the arrival of my daughter. With the book in my hand, I count my steps, five paces to the left, and five paces to the right, anxiously tapping the book against my chest.

"That's it. Today has to be the day." I say aloud on my last step to the left.

"What has to be today?" Lindsey's voice calls from the bottom of the porch steps.

"Oh dear, I didn't hear you arrive." I turn to face my daughter's voice. "I was thinking how nice it would be to stop by the hydroponics store and get some flowers to bring to Dee."

Surely, Lindsey can't tell I'm trying to cover up my secret. Can she? Lindsey is already overly protective of me. These days it seems Lindsey is more of the mother figure in our relationship. At times, it frustrates me but it is the circle of life, I suppose.

"Okay, let me help you." Lindsey touches my hand and guides me down the steps. "One, Two, and..."

"I know how to walk," I snap, my frustration apparent in my voice. I regret it the second my temper flares.

I can feel her hands loosen from mine. She doesn't let go, just relaxes enough to make it known that she's only trying to help. Amazing how my other senses have become so much stronger since my sight started to go.

After a moment, I relax. "I'm sorry dear, your mother is getting old and not liking it much." I pat her hand.

"Mom, I guess we *both* have to get use to aging stuff. I'm not all that far behind you, remember."

Lindsey rubs my frail shoulders. I was always a tall woman. Over the years, I'm not so notably tall, though. Each inch went with each year that passed.

Doctor's said, "It's common as we age. Our bones become brittle and lose strength."

I just accepted that as my fate, again something already put into place for me. *Whatever...*

The doors of the hover car open as we approach the vehicle. Ashley's small voice sings from the back seat. "Hi, Grammy."

"Oh, hi sweetie," I answer. "No school today?"

"Mommy said I could stay home because my belly hurts." She giggled. "At least it hurt this morning. I'm all better now."

I can hear Ashley's small voice humming a song. I recognize it as a song I sang to Lindsey as a little girl. I would sing it as I combed her hair in the evenings.

"What are you doing, sweetie?" I asked as the car's harness wrapped me into my seat. I can sense Ashley's movement in the back seat behind me.

"I'm brushing my dolly's hair, Grammy." Ashley continued the song but this time with words.

"Twinkle, twinkle, little star. How I wonder what you are. Up above the world so high. Like a diamond in the sky."

A smile spreads across my face. At this very moment, I see again, how I will live on even after I am gone. *Just like the stars.*

***

The hover car pulls into the wrap-around driveway of the nursing home. A slight fluttering dances in my belly then moves its way to my chest.

I'm excited, but a hint of fear waves past me, only for a moment. *How will I find my way? I can't see...*

The sound of the automatic doors opening and the safety harness releasing, make the fear disappear.

"Hello, Mrs. Watson. Glad you made it today. Ms. Deidra is waiting for you in the garden. We put her next to the vortex fountain. I thought the sound of the water would be stimulating."

Nurse Kathy touches my hand to help me out of the hover car. "She was looking for her again...," she whispers into my ear. "Seems every week she has these spells the night before your arrival... and then after you come, she is content again..."

I just smile toward the foggy-faced redhead Kathy. *Oh if they only knew...*

"Can you keep a secret?" I whisper back. "We are going to find her today." I hold the book tighter today than ever before.

"See you at three, Mother," Lindsey yells from the car.

"Bye, Grammy. Have fun!" little Ashley's voice follows.

I smile and wave to the sound of their voices. I turn toward the entrance of the nursing home and Nurse Kathy leads me into the building.

The smell of old people is stronger today than most days. There isn't enough menthol or antiseptic to cover up the smell of decaying bodies. The smell sits around the recreational hall playing cards and board games.

I can hear a few of the old folks hooked up to those virtual living simulators, a headpiece they use for dementia patients to help them with the memories of things they have lost or think they've lost.

They tried it a few times with Dee, but she didn't respond, so they discontinued that therapy on her.

My visits and the book are the only thing Dee responds to. Even if it is only a twitch of an eye, slightest nod of the head and her so called episodes or spells.

"Just a little farther, Mrs. Watson," Nurse Kathy said as we zig zagged through the tables of old people.

I can't see them but I sure can smell them.

"It's a beautiful day to be in the garden," she added as she opened the exit door. The warmth of the sunshine blasts me in the face. The aroma of the flowers dances its way to my nose as if to tell me "hello."

"Oh dear, I left the flowers in the car that I brought for Dee. They were roses."

Nurse Kathy led me to Dee's droid wheel chair.

"How do I get this thing to work? If we decide to take a walk?" I ask.

"This button here moves forward and this is reverse. It has sensors that beep to keep it from bumping into things. The voice recognition talks you through the direction you are heading. Mrs. Deidra could probably drive the thing herself if she would just try." Nurse Kathy laughs.

"If you have trouble just press the button right here..." She placed my hand on the button. "It will signal for me and I'll find ya."

"Thank you," I say and then the sound of the vortex fountain catches my attention. Suction of air and water into something unknown. It has to be a beautiful sight.

After nurse Kathy leaves the two of us alone, I bend down to Dee's ear and whisper, "We are going on an adventure today..."

I lay the book in Dee's lap. I feel my way around the chair and grip the handles as tight as I can–and I exhale.

I press the forward button down and off we go. I can see the shadowy image of Dee bouncing in the chair from the garden terrain. The chair is moving almost too fast for me to keep up.

"We are going to find Lizzy today, Dee," I gasp as I stumble and the chair's motions pulls me so quickly I lose my footing.

The chair drags me to the ground. I reach for the button and my head slams to the ground, right on top of a rock by the feel of it.

The chair moves forward. "Ohhh..."

CHAPTER FOURTEEN

LIZZY'S EMPTY SAC

"I will love them and reveal myself to them."-John 14:21

2004

Lizzy woke as the sun was coming up. She was not an early riser but she couldn't sleep. With everything that had happened in the past few days her brain was on overload.

The conversation with Henry's father *Alo*; the news of Gracey's cancer; the time she'd spent in Joe's arms; all of it, connected by love. *The love for one another that we sometimes don't see until it's laid out in front of us, demanding to be seen.*

I am okay with being alone. She had an overwhelming feeling of appreciation and was actually content with her quiet home. She now believed the quiet was only temporary. *A season that will pass. Just as all seasons do.* She needed to embrace it because before too long a child would be filling the void. Which also made her realize if she was going to write a book she needed to get as much written before the baby came-right?

Lizzy thought back to the conversation she'd had with Dee. Dee had told her Henry wanted to bring a butterfly to her property and release it. He told Dee the butterfly was in memory of the child she had lost. It was a beautiful thought and Lizzy loved things that held meaning. How ironic that the poem she had written to her unborn child held the phone number to Henry's father. There was no doubt in her mind that God had played a part in what was happening. Which too, gave her comfort.

Today Lizzy was going to the doctor and having her first sonogram. She still debated on finding out the sex of the baby. *Could I keep the secret?* Lizzy giggled.

Moments later, she stood from the couch and walked to the kitchen. She sat her coffee mug in the sink. Ripley came to mind. *We should have that picnic by the lake, too.*

"I'll give Ripley a call, tell Dee, too. It will be like old times. The three of us getting together." Another epiphany. "The kids can go fishing. I'll pick up some boiled peanuts." Lizzy grinned. The plans of their gathering made her almost forget the time. *Got to get ready. Doctor wants me early for blood work.*

An hour later Lizzy sat on the table in the sonogram room wearing nothing but her undies and a paper gown. She glanced around the room at all the picture of fetuses and the different stages of gestation.

The nurse entered the room. "Hello, my name is Tara. I will be giving you your sonogram today. Are you ready to get started?" She smiled.

"Yep," Lizzy answered and shuffled a little making the paper crinkle underneath her bottom.

"Lie back and get comfortable."

Nurse Tara dimmed the lights. She sat down at the monitor and typed information onto a key board. She grabbed a remote and clicked on a TV that was just above where Lizzy laid.

"You can get a look at your baby from that screen." She stood, pulled up the paper gown to expose Lizzy's belly. She squirted some gel-like substance on to Lizzy's baby bump. "You ready?" She smiled, then lifted the sonogram camera. She placed it on Lizzy's belly and rolled it around.

"Hmmm...three sac's," she mumbled. "Two fetuses."

"What's that mean?" Lizzy asked, wishing Joe was with her.

"You are going to have twins," Tara said. "There is an extra sac. Three sacs."

"Twins?" Lizzy started to sit up and stopped herself. "What is the third sac?"

"Possibly *was* a third child. It occurs thirty percent of the time in multiple pregnancies."

"Twins?" Lizzy asked again.

"Congratulations! You are having two babies." Tara smiled but continued to roll the camera around.

"Are they healthy? What does 'empty sac' mean?"

"Vanishing Twin syndrome. Usually happens in the first trimester of a multiple pregnancy. Also called *fetal resorption*. Your body will absorb it." She moved the camera over top of the empty sac and clicked. "It often occurs when... let's put it like this: The fertilized egg wasn't healthy, so it never developed, which in return made these two babies, Baby One..." she clicked an arrow over top of the picture on the screen, "And Baby Two," she clicked again, "healthier with a better chance to survive."

"Are they healthy?" Lizzy asked again, feeling her heartrate pick up.

"They look really good. Measurements are on target." Tara stopped realizing Lizzy had a tear running down her cheek and her bottom lip tucked under her teeth. "Oh, dear. Honey it is nothing to worry over. I promise. The doctor will monitor you even closer now. Everything looks really good."

"I lost my first child from a miscarriage," Lizzy whimpered. "I just got scared for a moment."

"These babies are fine, from what I can see. Healthy heartbeats," Tara confirmed. The sound of two heartbeats echoed as the camera moved across Lizzy's belly.

"Babies...." Lizzy sighed dreamily. "Twins." She glowed as another tear fell.

Today her tears were happy ones.

***

After Lizzy finished with her doctor's appointment, the excitement of *twins* was about to spill over. Joe sounded like he was ready to jump through the phone to come home.

She stopped by the Bantam Chef for one of their famous fish sandwiches. It was huge and delicious. Lizzy was fond of the place because as a very young child she remembered having lunches there with her father; a root beer float with a Chuck Wagon sandwich to be exact.

Today she was just going to grab a sandwich to go and get to BUCKETS. The news of twins was killing her–she needed to tell Dee.

"Thank you." Lizzy grabbed the brown paper bag from the window and walked back to her Jeep. The fragrance of the fried fish snuck out of the bag.

Only a week ago the smell of fish would have made her barf but today it was calling her name. The doctor said too much fish wasn't good for the babies but occasionally it was okay. It had something to do with the mercury that fish carried.

Once she arrived at BUCKETS, she got out of the Jeep and made her way to the front door, swinging the paper bag as if it held the secret. She opened the door to BUCKETS and saw Dee standing at the register babbling to herself about remembering to talk to Lizzy about this weekend.

"Hey," Lizzy interrupted. She knew her smile was almost as big as the fish sandwich she couldn't wait to sink her teeth in. "Just got back from my sonogram."

Dee turned to the register. "And?"

"Everything looks good. The babies are healthy." Lizzy smiled even bigger this time.

"Babies?" Dee squealed.

"Yep!" Lizzy sat her Bantam chef bag on the bar top.

"I knew it!" Dee slapped both hands on the bar top on each side of the brown paper bag. "I freaking knew it! Are they girls?"

"Oh, it's too early to tell their sex." Lizzy pulled out the stool and worked around her belly to get into it. "I have had this overwhelming craving for a Bantam Chef fish sandwich."

"Fish? I thought the smell of fish was making you sick?" Dee laughed.

"It *was*...I am a mess, Dee." Lizzy unwrapped the sandwich from the wax paper and began to babble. "Sad one day. Happy the next. I can't stand fish. Then feel like I'm going to die if I don't eat it. Doctor says I only have a few months before he suggests no work and bed rest. I'm going to go insane."

"Here." Dee threw down an Adult Community Education newsletter; classes of all sorts were listed. "Take a class. You have always said you wanted to go back to school."

Lizzy thumbed through the newsletter and noticed a class on writing novels. She always loved writing and she *was* writing in her journal. She vowed to herself, she was going to write a book.

Come to find out the instructor of the class owned his own publishing company. Lizzy read it repeatedly, really considering taking the class.

At that exact moment, the front door opened. Lizzy lifted her sandwich to her mouth and glanced at the arriving customer. Tall, dark and handsome man.

She looked up at Dee whose eyes were normal. Dee's expression quickly changed into shock and surprise.

Lizzy took a huge bite just as the realization entered her head. This was Henry's father.

"Oh dear..." Lizzy mumbled through the fish sandwich.

CHAPTER FIFTEEN

DEE'S NIGHT OUT

"Sometimes a short walk down memory lane is all it takes to appreciate where you are today."-Susan Gale

2004

"Deidra?"

In a split second, moments of that night raced through Dee's memory. The night of pure passion with no endings of heartache. Every sexy detail. Dee stood frozen.

"Alo. My name is Alo. We met a few years back. Right here. Bike week." He glanced around and chuckled. "This exact spot." His hands rubbed the bar top as if he felt energy that was powerful and passionate; in the exact place, he sat during Bike Week five years ago. He looked up at Dee. "You look just as beautiful as I remember."

"I'm sorry. I just..." Dee stuttered. "I do remember you..."

Lizzy swallowed and cleared her throat. "Hi I'm Lizzy. I'm the one that called you," she said from the other end of the bar.

"Yes. Hello, again," he answered not taking his eyes off Dee. "I have thought about you almost daily since that night..."

"Dee. I go by Dee, not Deidra." She smiled, not knowing how to act but simply like a barmaid would. She threw a coaster on top of the bar. Put her finger to her lips and tapped them. "Bud, right?" She asked trying to be nonchalant.

"You remember? I mean... you remember me?" he asked.

"I do..." Was all she could say. *Think Dee. Don't scare him away.*

"Yes, a Bud will do." He sat on the exact stool he had occupied that glorious night.

Breathe, Dee. Dee opened the bottle and placed it in front of him. "You still ride?" she asked, still attempting to be nonchalant.

"I'll always ride." He smiled and sipped his beer watching her the whole time.

Dear God, is he thinking what I'm thinking? Each second Dee stared at him the memory of that night flashed in her mind. *Bonnie and Clyde.* She was not the same person as she was that night. *Or am I?* So much had changed since then. She was a mother now. She had responsibilities to live up to. She had Henry to protect.

"Would you consider another ride?" he asked.

Ohhhh, he is thinking what I'm thinking. "I'd love to," she blurted out. *Oh dear what about Henry?* Dee looked swiftly at Lizzy then back at Alo.

"Dee, can I talk to you a minute?" Lizzy interrupted. She made her way to the kitchen holding her stomach as if something was wrong.

"Is she okay?" Alo asked gently.

"I should probably go see if she is." Dee smiled and left the bar rag on the bar. She trailed behind Lizzy.

"I can get Henry from the day care. Angel will be here soon," Lizzy whispered. "I'll just take Henry back to my house. Get to know this guy first, Dee. Remember to go with your gut."

That was every problem that Dee needed to solve and Lizzy had wrapped it all up in a second.

"It's not my gut I'm worried about," Dee whispered through her teeth with a giant grin. "Every ounce of my being is tingling for this man. What if I can't hear what my gut is saying?"

"He *is* handsome," Lizzy whispered. "So have some fun, then. Give it time. Don't rush the Henry news." Lizzy paused. "Yet." She held up her pointer finger.

"You're right. I'll get to know him first." Dee shook her head. "Kind of ironic, isn't it? The first time I met him I just wanted to have fun. No strings, you know? I'd already lost so many when he came around." She poked her head out of the kitchen doorway to glance out at the bar, and then returned. "Now I feel like I want to reel him in slow and easy, like a fish, hoping the line doesn't break."

Lizzy pushed Dee out of the kitchen. "Go. I have you covered tonight." Dee walked back to the bar and replaced empty bottles with fresh ones for some of the customers that were becoming part of the BUCKETS family.

"How is your friend? Lizzy is it?" Alo asked as Dee wiped the bar top next to him.

"Oh, she's fine. Pregnant. She ate a huge fish sandwich. The whole fish sandwich." Dee glanced where Lizzy had sat moments before. "That fish sandwich is legendary around here. Not many people can eat the whole thing." Again Dee babbled to not look so freaking attracted to him.

"So what time do you get off?" Alo asked. He leaned across the bar and whispered, "I'm staying up at the same hotel that we stayed in that night...same room, too."

Dee grinned. All she could do was grin.

Bonnie and Clyde.

Nooo...Scarlett O'Hara and Rhett Butler.

Better yet, Odysseus and Penelope. He will have to prove he is worthy.

***

After Angel had arrived and Lizzy headed to get Henry, all of Dee's responsibilities were in the hands of someone else. This gave her a guilty feeling of freedom. Exciting it was to have a little adventure. Part of her brain coached rational and the other part screamed adventure. She was always about adventure.

When Henry was born, her life had become more about rational and the best decisions. She quickly pushed the thought aside, at least for the moment. She grabbed her backpack from the coat hook.

"Okay, Angel, are you all good?"

"I think so." Angel smiled.

"If you have a problem or need anything...Don't call me." Dee laughed. "Call Lizzy."

Yep, she was going to make the most of her evening. From the look on Angel's face, she must have been due for some Dee-time.

Alo had mentioned getting showered up and meeting Dee at the bar at the edge of town. The same bar where the local bikers gathered for their monthly poker runs. It was just as well, it was a halfway point from Dee's home and the hotel. The hotel where he was staying. She would have her truck this time, and she could stay or she could go. It was the feeling of choice that eased her mind.

In less than an hour, Dee showered and headed back to her truck. She pulled out of the drive to meet the sexy biker. Black tank top, blue jeans, and her black riding boots joined the adventure. A hint of perfume and a smile of need included, as an extra. Music blasted from the radio, "Born to be Wild" by Steppenwolf, to be exact.

Two miles later, Dee turned down the music as she rolled into the bar's parking lot. *Oh dear, with all of the excitement I've almost forgotten. He is Henry's father...*

For a moment Dee realized she was being selfish, only thinking of how this man affected *her*. She desperately needed to see how he would be for Henry's sake.

She got out of the truck looked in the mirror, added a little lip-gloss and closed the truck door. Her red hair waved wild and unmanageable, just like she felt. *Okay Dee, work your magic.*

Dee had always had a way with men. She had an affect on them that was almost hypnotic, Lizzy used to tell her. The less Dee tried the more they wanted her.

She entered the smoke-filled bar. The live band played on the stage in the corner. The music pounded, upbeat and fell into rhythm to her heartbeat. She spotted Alo standing at the bar, in the same spot as they had stood that night. Which to Dee showed he was very set in his ways.

Dee always believed that she could tell a person by how they entered a room. If a person returned to the same spot when they entered, they were grounded and constant. If they entered and looked around, they were in search of something. Which was exactly what *she* had done.

If a person entered a room and moved about to find the perfect seat they were unreliable and never content. That was her strange creed. It always seemed to be pretty accurate, though.

Alo's back faced her direction. He stood gorgeous, even from behind. He slowly turned as if he sensed she had arrived. Like he could feel her arrival. The music stopped and so did time. The soft sound of a love song started to play.

"Let's slow this down a bit, grab that special someone," the DJ announced as the stage light darkened to relieve the band. The lights dimmed on the dance floor and the disco ball spotted tiny lights across the room like twinkling stars.

Alo made eye contact with Dee. The right corner of his mouth lifted to show his beautiful smile emerging. *Henry has his smile. That alone could cause me to fall in love.* He nodded his head towards the dance floor. No words, just a silent suggestion. Dee gestured yes. He moved towards her and grabbed her hand. He pulled her onto the dance floor and wrapped her in his sculpted arms, as he began to move to the music.

Oh he smells so good. Fresh, clean and minty. He wore a black tank top too, with faded Levi's that fit perfectly. His tan skin glistened in the light of the disco ball. He wore his long hair in a tightly braided ponytail, sleek and shiny. The amazing artwork along his exposed arms looked just as Dee had remembered.

Without realizing it, she reached her hand to admire them with her fingertips. *Tribal tattoos for sure.* She gently outlined the tattoo of the hunch back figure that held the whistle. As if it was something that had meaning to her.

In a way, it did have meaning; the story of the pied piper as a little girl and the memory of Henry with the whistle in the garden. Dee knew from her American Indian culture studies that everything had meaning.

After being mesmerized by the tattoo, she heard him whisper into her ear, "Kokopelli, God of love," almost as if he knew what she had been thinking. He whispered again. "My people believe he is the bringer of the new season."

"The new season?" Dee wondered if he could read her thoughts.

"There are many myths. My favorite is that he traveled from village to village bringing the changing of winter to spring." He swayed with the music almost hypnotizing Dee. Her hips followed with his. His warmth radiated off his body as if she could feel winter becoming spring. She looked up to his face and listened more.

"Melting the snow and bringing about rain for a successful harvest." He smiled at Dee as if he sensed her intrigue.

"It's amazing." She traced it again with her finger and stopped at the hunch in his back.

"The hunch on his back depicted the sacks of seeds and songs he carried with him on his travels. Kokopelli's flute is said to be heard in the spring's breeze, while bringing warmth to the gardens."

The music continued as they moved together, slow and smooth. His voice was almost as musical as the flute Dee had imagined Kokopelli to play.

"Legend has it, everyone in the village would sing and dance throughout the night when they heard Kokopelli play his flute. The next morning, every maiden in the village would be with child," he added.

Henry...

The music ended and a fast pace music began to play. The dim lights were now flashing with upbeat energy. *Ohhh boy. This is so surreal.* Everything was making her have some sort of understanding. It was always her fate. She needed to know more about this man. *Henry's father, he was and was always supposed to be.*

"What's your nationality? I'm assuming American Indian?" Dee yelled over the music, as they moved from the dance floor and back to their place at the bar.

"Yes, Hopi tribe are my people. We are one of the few tribes recognized by the national government. Our land is in Arizona."

How ironic that she had always had a fascination with American Indian beliefs and her mother and father, too. Is it that we connect to these things for reason, or is it the reason we become connected? She had a child with this man, yet knew nothing about him. Now somehow it was meant to be. As if remembering him somehow?

"Alo is the name my people gave me at birth." He added. "Meaning, spiritual guide."

Dee just smiled at him. She knew for sure he was supposed to be Henry's father. She was always into spiritualism from the moment as a small child. She was seeing connection to the man. A connection that made their first meeting make all kinds of sense.

"Two beers, please" Alo yelled to the bartender.

Dee stayed silent but her brain worked overtime.

He turned to her. "I'm sorry; I just keep feeling like we only left off, where we ended. Is beer good for you?"

"I guess we kind of did...only four...five years later."

She really needed to tell him about Henry. He was a good man. Henry needed to know his father. Henry needed to know his people.

CHAPTER SIXTEEN

RIPLEY AND DEE'S ADVENTURE

"No pessimist ever discovered the secret of the stars, or sailed to an uncharted land, or opened a new doorway for the human spirit."-Helen Keller

2050

"Rip? Are you all right? Ripley?" A muffled voice asked becoming clearer in the darkness. My old tired eyes slowly opened.

"If you can't beat'em, join'em I always say." Above me stood a foggy version of an old silver headed Dee. As I started to sit up, my sight slowly focused on the person standing in front of me. It was Dee, and she was coherent. She stood talking to me.

"I can see you," I gasped. "I can see...and you...you are here."

"Are you all right? You took a nasty fall," Dee remarked as she helped me to my feet. She brushed at the leaves that were clinging to my pants.

"You're really here and I can *see* you." I exhaled the disbelief. I glanced around. We were no longer at the nursing home and I had my vision back. We were standing in a strange wooded forest. *Are we in the bayou? Where are we? Am I dreaming?*

"We aren't dreaming," Dee said.

She hears what I'm thinking?

"I do." Dee grinned. "Can't keep no secrets from me. At least *here* you can't."

"I'm confused," I confessed.

"Are we gonna have some fun or what? I've been cooped up with old people for way too long. By the way, thanks for reading to me every Wednesday. That was the only sanity I could get in that place." Dee just grinned.

"Where are we?" I looked around not recognizing anything.

"The Mystical Forest. I come here a lot. More so now." Dee patted me on the back and strolled around a birch tree. "You gave this back to me. When you started reading to me, it helped me remember this place. Cool, right?"

Dee picked at her teeth with a twig she had scooped up from the ground. With each step she took, her silver hair started to recolor itself to the most beautiful shade of red I had ever seen. The worn, tired eyes she bore too began to smooth out. In very little time, she looked just as she had when we were young women.

"You are...young." I stumbled over my words. "I can see you, and you're young."

"We...we my dear, are young."

I looked down at my hands. My hands reminded me so much of how my mother's hands looked just a few years before she had passed. The age spots lightened and the creases and wrinkles straightened with each blink of my tired eyes. I slowly stood straight and I no longer had a slouching posture. *I feel amazing.* Every ache, every stiff part of my body was gone. *I too, am young again.*

"So you want to live, right?" Dee smiled. "Let's get the hell on with it then." She grabbed me by the hand and pulled me along towards the beautiful rainbow that stood at the edge of the forest.

"Wait, we need to grab the book." I glanced back to where the droid chair sat moments before. The book was no longer there.

"We don't need the book now..." Dee just smiled at me. "We are *in* it. Come on... let's get to the Garden...Lizzy should be there. Oh boy do I have a surprise for you..."

***

"What is happening here?" I asked as we walked through the rainbow, into a field of sunflowers and daisies. Each flower pivoted towards the suns beautiful light, as if time was moving in fast forward, yet standing still at the same moment. "Sunflowers and daisy's together." I admired the sight.

"Sunflowers and daisies are part of the same family. They represent loyal love. The 'Asteraceae' is the largest flowering plant family and the name means, star." Dee smiled. "Star family," she added as she touched the giant sunflower cupping it in her hand.

"Absolutely beautiful." I admired the beautiful flowers.

"We are special Ripley. We were born as what they call star children. We were placed on earth to change things. To help people. Like Earth angels." Dee glanced at me as she moved the massive sunflowers out of our walking path, but the daisies remained. "We are good. We help people see things that are unseen. Like wireless internet." Dee smiled.

"I don't understand."

"Remember when cell phones, wireless technology, and cordless phones came to be? We had to try to explain how it worked to your parents, right? How information was all around us but yet they didn't see it." Dee stopped walking for a moment.

"I guess. I still don't understand what that has to do with what is happening with us, here. Now."

"That is exactly what is happening to us. Our brain is made up of energy that I call my soul, you call your conscience, and Lizzy called it her muse. Like cellular energy or wireless internet. Love is that connection, an unconditional connection. Our bodies are only the vessel, like the phone. The phone helps retrieve the signal."

"So, are you saying we aren't in our vessels right now? We are only energy waves? Connected by unconditional love?"

"Exactly! Star children are those that know they are connected through these energy waves. You've heard the saying kindred souls, right? There is no cord that holds us together. Only an invisible thread, an energy wave of unconditional love." Dee began to walk again.

"We are only a small part of a bigger something. Each of us has our own function. Like this book, we are the characters, each of us different, but connected, we make up the story." Dee stopped again and tapped her pointer finger to her lip three times. "Kind of like cells in your body. They all work to help the body function or the vessel per say."

"I kind of understand. I guess what I'm really wanting to know is... Where is my vessel? Are we dead?"

"Rip, I'm as healthy as a horse, you heard the doctors. It's going to take more than you having a nasty fall to kill me off." Dee grinned. "Your vessel is fine, and you aren't dead. They...I'll explain more of that to you later. For now, let's go live. We might even get a chance to visit with Lizzy."

"But...I thought...So Lizzy is...she's here?"

"No, not really *here*. Like I said, we're all a part of a bigger whole. She isn't here, but we are there. I know I'm probably confusing the hell out of you. We are in the book, remember?"

Dee always had a way with words. Although at times they were complicated and eccentric, her ideas always helped me see things I would have never have noticed or seen if it was not for Dee. Dee sometimes even helped me understand the wrongs of the world, and how maybe the wrongs weren't so wrong; how everything had a consequence, a reason or a function.

"Speaking of Lizzy, remember back before Lizzy moved in with us? How we use to know how each other felt, and would answer each other before the question was asked? We were connected then." Dee smiled.

"Remember in Mrs. Lily's 1st grade art class? You, me and Lizzy all painted similar garden pictures. Connected!" Dee squealed and then she continued.

"We weren't friends back then but we were all three connected. Almost like we knew we would always meet in the garden." Dee smiled with a confirming nod. "Oh yeah, and when Lizzy moved back into town? You said yourself you knew she was back before you even called her parent's home. You said you felt her presence. Remember? Bam! Connected!"

"I was never good at remembering that kind of stuff," I said. "Honestly only recently have I been flooded with all kinds of memories. I gave credit to the book."

"Oh yes, the book. Kind of funny, isn't it? You say you want to live, yet every time the book is read you *are* living. In whoever is reading the book, you are living in their imagination. You will live *forever*."

"It isn't the same."

Dee stepped over top of some old railroad tracks that the sunflowers had grown to cover up. I followed her. "Oh but it is the same." Dee grinned and stopped staring ahead. "I wanted to stop by here to see how the old house was doing."

Only a short distance away stood the old house Dee was so very fond of. She had inherited it after her father died. She always talked about having some connection to it, even before she learned her family owned it. *Maybe she's right about being linked through unconditional love.*

The house stood just as I remembered. I too, always loved that old house. As to why? Probably the stories that seemed to come from it. Mostly ghost stories. I never believed there were ghost but Dee's theory of energies somehow made the house and the stories all make some sort of crazy sense. A lot like my old sofa and the memories that still sat upon it.

"Let's go check it out. It should only take a minute." Dee grabbed for my hand. "A minute," Dee huffed. "I always forget time doesn't exist here." She dragged me by the hand toward the old house.

CHAPTER SEVENTEEN

LIZZY WORRIES

"Like good stewards of the manifold grace of God, serve one another with whatever gift each of you has recieved."-1 Peter 4:10

2004

Lizzy woke and glanced at Henry still peacefully sleeping. *How adorable he is.* For a moment, the concern of Dee's night projected to Lizzy, a vision of comfort for dear Henry. *He finally gets to meet his father. Things must have went well.* Movement came from Henry and both Bella and Tank ears went up as if waiting for Henry to wake. Both dogs' tails began to tap the hardwood floor.

"Shhh...don't wake him," Lizzy whispered to Tank and Bella. She knew how excited they were to have Henry stay the night. Lizzy and Henry both had slept on the couch in the living room, just to stay close to the dogs. They adored the special little boy.

Lizzy tip toed to the kitchen and made herself a cup of coffee. *Only one.* No matter how tempting that second cup appeared to be, she stuck to her doctor's orders. She sipped. She decided to give Ripley a call. In addition, to remind her of the weekend picnic she had planned. She picked up the phone and began to dial. After the third ring Ripley answered.

"Hey Ripley, I wanted to see if you and Lindsey wanted to come by this Saturday. Dee's coming with Henry. She's gonna finish mowing the pasture for Joe. We can have a picnic," she explained. "I thought the kids would get a kick out of fishing."

Lizzy listened more. "No, I have it covered," she responded to Ripley. She did a quick glance into the living room at Henry, who was still asleep on the couch. "Yeah it will be like old times." Lizzy smiled. "Okay I'll see you then." She hung up the phone and sipped her coffee.

"Aunt Izzy?" Henry's small voice startled her and she turned toward it. "My tummy hurts and I want my mommy." Henry stood with the most adorable grimace on his face.

"Oh, honey..." Lizzy bent to his level. "How about I make you some toast?"

"Okay, then I go see my mommy?" he asked.

"I need to call her first," Lizzy tried to explain. "I told her I would take you to your school this morning because I have to open BUCKETS."

What do I do now? Lizzy popped two pieces of toast in the toaster and grabbed the butter from the fridge. "Let's get you some toast. You want a glass of milk?" She looked down at Henry and his grimace. He was still holding his tummy.

The toast popped up from the toaster and she buttered both pieces. "Would you like some grape jelly on it?"

"No yelly." Henry still grimaced.

His tummy is really bothering him. He always wants jelly. "Okay, come sit and eat while I give your mom a call." Lizzy took Henry's toast to her dining room table as he followed. He sat still staring at the toast and holding his belly. Lizzy went to the kitchen and grabbed the jar of jelly and a butter knife. *Just in case.* He picked the toast up and took a bite. Lizzy watched until he took the second bite.

She picked up the phone and dialed Dee's phone number. After moments of ringing, the answering machine picked up.

"Hey Dee, it's me, Henry has a tummy ache. I don't know if I should take him to school...Call me...I might just bring him with me to BUCKETS. Please just give me a call. I honestly don't know what I should do." Lizzy hung up the phone. *She must still be with Alo.*

"How is your tummy?" Lizzy walked back over to the dining room table.

"My mommy didn't answer? Where did she go again?" Henry looked up at Lizzy with Jelly all over his face.

"You changed your mind about the jelly I see." Lizzy stood above him with her hands on her hips. "Your mommy had to meet with somebody."

"My daddy..." Henry blurted as a fact. *How did he know? I never said anything to him.*

"Possibly. What makes you think this?" Lizzy asked sitting down beside him at the table.

"I just know." Henry picked up his glass of milk and chugged some down. He wore a milk mustache as he took another bite of toast.

This kid is simply amazing.

"I see him... Sometimes in my dreams," Henry continued. "He just stands and watches me play in the garden. He doesn't talk to me, just watches."

"Really?" Lizzy placed her fist under her chin to prop her head up to listen more. Henry intrigued her. Lizzy always believed Dee had something intuitive about her and now Henry too was showing signs.

***

Lizzy pulled the Jeep into BUCKETS. She still had not heard from Dee, which began to make her worry. She decided not to take Henry to school and just bring him to BUCKETS. Dee was bound to be calling soon. Or so she hoped.

She unbuckled Henry from his car seat. "Henry, Aunt Lizzy needs you to climb down. I'll help you."

"We don't want to hurt da babies," Henry mumbled as he climbed down from his seat. "Aunt Izzy, I really want my mommy."

"I know honey, she should be here soon. I promise." Another reason Lizzy did not want to take him to school. He was really missing his mother. Lizzy did not want him to worry at school. *He can worry with me.*

As she unlocked the door to BUCKETS. She made her way to the alarm and typed in the code. Henry followed. The phone rang.

"That's probably your mommy now." Lizzy waddled her way to the phone as Henry stood holding a color book and crayons.

"BUCKETS, may I help you?" Lizzy answered. "I have him here." She glanced a Henry and mouthed *It's your mommy.*

"I didn't know what I should do..." Lizzy smiled at Henry. "His tummy is a little better." She listened. "Okay. No problem. He can color till you get here," Lizzy whispered so Henry could not hear. "Did you tell Alo yet?"

Lizzy hung up the phone worried again, but relieved Henry could stop worrying.

"She'll be here in about thirty minutes. Climb on the stool and color while I get the bar ready to open."

Gosh, I never asked Dee how the night went. Maybe that's why she hasn't told him about Henry.

***

Lizzy busied herself getting BUCKETS ready to open. While Henry colored in his coloring book, Italian lentil soup steamed hot and fresh from the stove. Joe's mother had given her the recipe. The customers seemed to love it and Dee called it her favorite too. It was garlic, lentils, spinach, Italian sausage crumbs, and pasta in a chicken broth. Served with parmesan cheese on top and cheesy garlic bread.

It was one of Joe's, family's traditional meal for New Year's Day. Although it was not New Years, it seemed to be a start of a "new something." There was a meaning to the soup, a lot like Lizzy's southern, traditional, New Year's meal. Lentils were for luck, verses Black eye peas. The spinach was for money, verses the collard greens in Lizzy's southern tradition.

Lizzy loved when things held a meaning. She thought in her own weird way, she would be serving a bit of luck and money to the customers-secretly. She grinned on the last stir of the soup.

"Mommy!" Henry's voice echoed.

Lizzy walked out of the kitchen and noticed Dee through the glass door about to enter BUCKETS, until a man stopped her. A worn, tired black man, with beads that looked like bones hanging around his neck. Dee nodded and straight faced gave the man another quick nod. *Who is that?*

She entered BUCKETS' front door looking distraught.

"No idea what that was about," she grumbled. "Very weird. Hey, sweetie," she said, shifting her expression as she made her way to Henry. "How's your tummy?"

"Much better. Aunt Izzy made me toast and it felt better." Henry colored a bit more, then picked up the picture he was working on. "Look! It's of you and Daddy."

Dee's face looked startled. Lizzy moved to view the picture and noticed the male in the picture *did* resemble Henry's father. *He has never even seen Alo! How does this child know what he looks like?* She and Dee stared at Henry.

At that very moment, the front door opened. Lo and behold, it was Alo, strolling in to have a beer. Lizzy's gaze shifted from Henry to Dee. *Uh-oh. If she hasn't mentioned Henry to Alo, she is going to have to now.*

Dee looked up, startled. "Alo."

Alo looked at Henry, then back at Dee. Lizzy could see his surprise. Henry smiled up at his father.

"He has my smile," Alo whispered to no one in particular.

Dee moved toward Alo to stop him from getting any closer to Henry. "Please let me explain..."

He pushed his way past her.

"I was going to tell you tonight..."

He walked to Henry who was still sitting on the stool. He cupped Henry's face.

"Hi, Daddy," said Henry as though he'd known Alo his entire life instead of sixty seconds.

Alo kissed Henry's forehead.

CHAPTER EIGHTEEN

DEE'S FEAR

"A mother's love for her child is like nothing else in the world. It knows no aw, no pity, it dares all things and crushes down remorselessly all that stands in its path."-Agatha Christie

2004

This isn't how I wanted this to happen. Dee watched as Henry greeted his father and Alo kissed his son's forehead for the first time. *Their instincts for each other are so surreal.*

Dee gazed at both of them then glanced at Lizzy who still stood with her mouth open but not saying a word. She seemed just as stunned as Dee felt.

I hope I haven't ruined this for Henry. Although, Henry did not seem to be the one whose relationship seemed ruined. After the kiss to Henry's forehead, Alo admired him for what seemed like hours to Dee, but only minutes passed. Then he stood with his shoulders back and did an about face, turning on his heels. He faced Dee.

"We need to talk. In private." Straight faced, he walked steadily out the door.

"I'm not leaving my son for you!" Dee yelled as the door closed behind him. She was not sure what she'd meant.

It wasn't supposed to happen like this! She'd truly fallen for this man. She already felt overwhelmed with guilt because she had left Henry last night. She was torn.

Then, the old black man with the bone necklace spooked her by saying *"We need the boy,"* moments before she entered BUCKETS. *What had he meant?* What was *all* of this meaning? Fear burrowed in her chest and she felt fear for the safety of her child. She felt a panic attack start to surface. She hadn't had one in years, but they'd almost destroyed her once upon a time.

Oh no...They are back. I can't lose Alo—it would devastate Henry. Dee's emotions warred in all directions.

"Take him to the garden, Dee." Lizzy's muffled voice sliced through the thickness of panic. "Beautiful things begin in the garden."

Dee inhaled a deep cleansing breath and held her finger in the air. "Could you watch him for just a minute?" Dee kissed Henry, not waiting for an answer from Lizzy.

She said to him, "Mommy will be right back, sweetie. I'm going to see if your daddy would like to come to the house with us."

"Yes, Mommy, the garden would be nice," he said, still smiling.

Dee agreed the garden was the perfect place. Besides being magical, the garden was also a place where Henry felt comfortable. All she had wanted was Henry to feel comfortable when he finally met his father. *He seems so content with all of this.*

Dee quickly marched out the door to face her fate or fears, too frazzled to know which it was.

She walked steadily toward him and his motorcycle. He stood with his back facing Dee, his head turned down.

I have disappointed him. She stood with her thumbnail planted behind her front teeth, not knowing what to say.

"Is that why she called me, Lizzy is it?" he asked softly.

"No... She really, accidently came across your number. It just happened...I swear."

"Was last night an accident, too?" His head dropped lower as he fumbled with the straps on his helmet.

"NO!" Dee jumped forward.

"Why didn't you tell me before...before everything that happened?" He finally turned to face her.

"I was being protective of Henry. It wasn't to hurt you...Or make you feel like you were being played. I wanted to be sure you were a good man...I did it all for Henry."

The silence stretched on as Alo's long, slender fingers continued to fidget with the helmet strap. Dee felt her heart breaking–she recognized the feeling from the past. She took a deep breath.

"Alo, I didn't know who you were–as a man, as a person," she rushed on. "One magical night wasn't enough for me to be sure."

His laugh was short, but not unkind. "I wanted more, Dee. Even back then." He shook his head. "So, now we've had two nights and you know me?" He lifted his gaze to meet hers.

She nodded. "As strange as that may sound, yes, I know enough. I've seen enough. I won't let you hurt Henry or me, either–but I don't think that's going to happen."

On the sidewalk that ran along the BUCKETS parking lot, a black women rode by on a three wheel bicycle staring at the two of them.

Dee watched her, some internal radar pinging a warning. Time began to slow. *"We need the boy,"* echoed out of the spokes of the bicycle as they spun past her in slow motion. Around the woman's neck hung a necklace just like the black man wore. Dee became spooked again and panic shot up her spine.

"Was last night for Henry?" Alo asked, his voice somehow making everything normal again.

She shook her head to rid the spell of the old woman. "No... Yes... No–I mean what happened between us was...I couldn't help it! I am so *damned* attracted to you. It started out *all* for Henry."

Dee began to pace. "I GOT SELFISH!" She threw her hands in the air and began to cry. "I wanted you for me, too."

In the midst of her tears, she pleaded, "Would you please just come to our house? Get to know us...For Henry's sake..."

***

The tears must have made Alo realize Dee was sincere. He mentioned he would meet them at their home but he wanted some time to think things through. To Dee it sounded reasonable. Part of her worried it was an excuse to escape and head back home to Arizona. Henry would be heartbroken....

Dee and Henry arrived home and Dee unbuckled Henry from his car seat and glanced across the street. Johnny had his election signs up in front of the shop.

A good and longtime friend, Johnny told Dee he was planning to run for city council after the last election. He and his wife Beth were now working on baby number two. Yep, Johnny and Beth had a little girl last year and not long after, Beth was pregnant again. Today he looked as though he was still chasing his butterflies.

"Mommy, when is Daddy going to come?" Henry held his mother's hand as they walked up to the front door of their home.

Dee worried that Henry would end up disappointed, so she answered, "When he is ready..."

She did not want to add the burden of what she had done, on to Henry. "Honey your daddy just found out he is your daddy. He didn't know Mommy had you. He needs time to let it soak in."

"Like when we water the garden?" Henry asked stopping at the front door. "Once the water soaks in, then it helps the flowers grow."

This child really is amazing...

"Exactly!" She rubbed Henry's head and opened the screen door. "After you, my handsome boy."

***

Dee paced for two hours in front of the picture window, waiting for Alo. *My directions were very precise.* She closed the blinds.

She decided to sit and try to relax. *He needs time to think, she* reminded herself for the eighth time. Henry sat on the living room floor playing with a puzzle.

"Honey, you've mastered that one. Maybe get another one to try."
Henry could have probably put that particular puzzle together with his
eyes closed.

He lifted his head and cocked it to one side. "You hear that
Mommy?" He got up and raced to the window. "He's coming." Henry
peeked through the blinds. "I don't see him, yet."

Dee spread the blind just enough to see the driveway and the road
out front. No sign of Alo, so she moved away from the window. *Poor
kid. He is so excited he's hearing things.* Just as she was about to
comfort him, she heard it, too. She stood beside her son, hoping they
wouldn't be disappointed.

The motorcycle zoomed into the driveway. Alo had arrived.

"He's here. He is here!" Henry ran to the front door and swung it
wide open. Dee followed. She stayed on the front porch watching
Henry run to his father.

Alo lowered the kickstand and removed his helmet. "Hey, Henry!
I got you a little something. I missed four birthdays, right?" He knelt
in front of the little boy with his hands on both knees.

"Yep." Henry grinned from ear to ear. "And I have another
coming dis year."

"Well, you'll have to wait for your birthday for that one."

Dee just stood on the porch with her arms lightly folded, smiling.
She stayed behind, letting the two of them get to know each other.
She glanced across the street where an old flat black Oldsmobile
rolled into Johnny's parking lot.

The tinted window rolled down and the Bone Man she'd met
outside of BUCKETS mouthed from the window, "We need the boy."

Panic washed over her. "Henry, Alo, please come inside." She eyed them, then glanced across the street and the car was no longer there. *I must be imagining these things.*

"Let me just get a few things from my saddle bags," Alo answered back. Dee's anxiousness was unnoticed.

Henry just stood hopping in one spot as he watched his father unload toys from his motorcycle.

Alo turned to Henry. "For your first birthday I missed..." He bent down to Henry and held out a necklace made of leather with what appeared to be something craved from a bone hanging from it. He placed it around his son's neck.

"Our people, the Hopi tribe, believe for the first birthday you get gifts from the family. It was mine, and my father gave it to me. His father gave it to him. It is a very old whistle made from an eagle's bone. It is said to play music beautiful enough to enchant the spirts." He slipped the leather cord over Henry's head, then stood.

"Okay let's go inside to see what else I have for you." Alo carried two bags toward the front door.

Henry stayed a moment and admired his necklace, then quickly caught up. Dee opened the door and held it for the two of them to enter. She glanced across the street and saw no sign of the black Oldsmobile.

Alo kissed Dee's cheek as he passed her. At that very moment everything seemed to be okay.

This just might work...

***

Alo and Henry sat on the floor of the living room. Dee stood watching as Henry opened each gift. He adored the tool set.

"Look, Mommy, they are real and not plastic." *Henry loves his tools...How could Alo have known?*

Henry loved the bug catcher and the bug habitat set. "We can catch Yoey with this and it won't hurt him...And this is much safer than that old jar." Dee watched the excitement that radiated off Henry. *He is so happy.*

"Wait!" Henry said, his face lighting up. "I have something for you, Daddy."

He stood and raced to his room. He returned seconds later with the Father's Day card he had made for his dad at preschool.

Alo took the card in his large hands as though it was made of spun glass. "Wow! You made this?" He stared down at the card. Glitter scattered when he opened it, like shooting stars.

Dee watched as Alo's eyes filled with tears. He glanced up at her and she just shrugged. What could she say? *She* knew how amazing Henry was. Alo had to experience it for himself.

The last gift was a bucket full of beach toys: shovel, rake, kite, and a beach towel. At the bottom was a bottle of bubbles.

"I thought maybe we could go to the beach one day." Alo said. "Only if your mommy says we can, though."

"Can she come too?" Henry asked.

"Sure, if she wants to." Alo gave Dee a nod.

Henry grabbed the bubbles and started to open them.

"Not in the house, Henry. Outside. You know the rule."

He gave Dee a mischievous grin. He stood, then went to the door and waited.

"Daddy, you coming?" Henry asked.

"Absolutely!" He gestured to Dee.

"Would you like some sweet iced tea?" she offered.

"I'd love some." He nodded again.

"Go on out to the garden, to the right of the porch. You'll see the stone path. You can sit on the swing. I'll be right out."

She peeked out the door to make sure the Oldsmobile was gone, then turned towards the kitchen. It was the first time she'd taken her eyes off Henry around Alo. She felt content with that, too. Henry always seemed to be a good judge of character. From what Dee could tell, Henry liked his father just as much as she did.

Moments later, she joined them in the garden. She held a tray with sweet tea and fruit slices on a plate. The sun shone brightly on the garden. The plants and flowers glistened with moisture from the watering earlier in the day.

Thank God Lizzy called Angel to come in and work for me. Everything is too perfect to have to run off to work. Gracey popped into her head for a moment. *I need to give her a call tomorrow to see how her doctor's visit went.*

"Mommy, watch this one!" Henry blew slowly into the bubble wand. A giant bubble made its way from the wand and floated across the garden. The butterflies fluttered around Henry, same as they had done that day with the flute-whistle.

Dee handed Alo his glass of tea and set the tray on the table next to the swing. She sat beside him.

"He is an amazing child." Alo sipped his tea. "He's a gift to this land."

They both sat a moment in comfortable silence. Dee began to speak as she reached for a slice of melon. "Is all of this going to change you and me?" she finally asked before biting into the sweet melon.

"Ha!" Alo leaned back on the swing. He cocked his head at Dee and smiled. "I was just asking myself the same exact thing." He turned his head toward Henry and smiled even wider. "I'll have to say...it spooked the hell outta me."

The swing swayed while Dee wiped the juice of the melon from her face. She began to speak again.

"I'm sorry you found out the way you did. I planned to tell you today and let you choose. I will admit Henry wanted to meet you and I was trying to remember whatever I could about you, just in case I was unable to find you. Then Lizzy called and said she had found your number. It was in her Bible..."

"Ahhh..., Christianity." Alo nodded as if confirming.

"Yes, Lizzy is a Christian."

"And you?" he asked.

"Well, my mother was raised Christian and we did attend a community church growing up. My parents actually met on the Seminole Indian reservation. The American Indian beliefs seemed to fit my father best.

"I believe... I am..." Dee laughed.

She honestly had never identified what she believed. Things were either good or they were bad. She believed in God or a great spirit and she believed Jesus was an example of who people should be.

Every belief system was the same to her; it was all in how people interpreted them. You were either good or you were bad. You were in charge of that, not your beliefs.

"I tend to believe too, as my father did. Kind of ironic, but the American Indian beliefs have always made the most sense to me."

"Ironic how?"

"I have an American Indian child. I wasn't even aware of it until this week. Now it all seems to come together and has reason. It all makes sense, now." She smiled at Alo.

"I have always believed things happen because they are supposed to. What belief is that called?" Dee pushed the swing with her foot and snickered.

"You are an amazing woman, Dee." Alo smiled.

"My father honestly practiced many beliefs, so trust me, American Indian beliefs became the winner." Dee stopped the swing with her foot. "It suited him." She noticed Henry talking to the butterfly with the broken wing. *Joey.* Which reminded her of their so-called *gift. I should just let Alo figure it out on his own.*

"I guess I believe in the spiritual aspect of all beliefs." Dee started the swing up again.

"Did I mention my name, Alo, means spiritual guide?"

"Ha, you did, didn't you!" Dee sat up from the swing and faced him.

"I can guide you, Dee," he whispered softly.

"Please do..." she whispered back.

CHAPTER NINETEEN

RIPLEY AND THE OLD HOUSE

"*A man must know his destiny, if he does not recognize it, then he is lost. By this I mean, once, twice, or at the very most, three times, fate will reach out and tap a man on the shoulder: if he has imagination, he will turn around and fate will point out to him what fork in the road he should take. If he has guts, he will take it."*-George S. Patton, Jr.

2050

I stood beside Dee in silence.

"I wish we could have done something with this old house," Dee said, standing on the front wooden steps looking up to the second story.

The old colored bottles still sat in the dust covered shadow box windows. The large oak tree's branch nearly touched the ground.

"You, me, and Lizzy...I wish we'd made it into a bed and breakfast. Maybe even a plant nursery. Hell, even a day care for kids.

Something. It had so much potential, but then the fire...” Dee's smile vanished.

“What fire? I don't remember any fire.” I glanced around at the old house. *It doesn't look as though there was any fire.*

“You don't remember or see it because Lizzy didn't write it in the book.” Dee turned away from me.

“That was the same time period we went our separate ways.” Dee strolled the porch. “So... She didn't write it... She wanted us to stay together, forever. And if she didn't write the fire in the book maybe...”

“Some stupid fire wouldn't have kept me from the two of you,” I said.

“It was more than just the fire and losing this old house. It was what we *all* lost at that time of our lives. The fire just happened. Rip, don't worry, it's not in the book. It's like it never happened.”

Dee rejoined me on the steps. “I don't remember a fire. Who or what did we lose? Why would we separate?”

“When it's time for you to know, you will. Come on, let's go in.”

Dee opened the wooden door and gestured to me to enter.

Inside the old house cobwebs stretched from corner to corner. Dust covered the hardwood floors. Each step we took, the dust parted, welcoming us.

I never believed in ghost or spirits, although, the house always felt like someone or something was there watching us. Never did I *see* any signs of ghost or spirits. And, I knew Dee did believe in such things.

Dee spun around in a circle like a little girl pretending to be a ballerina. "Things had to be much simpler for my Aunt Deidra and her friend Lizette. You know, running a tavern back in *those* days. Living upstairs and still caring for my father, they still had time to spend with Lizzy's grandmother," Dee babbled.

"Things were probably harder for them in other areas, like having the town accept them," I replied.

"Yeah that's true. I know Lizzy's grandma died not long after telling us about her connection to the two of them. Kind of like *us* being connected. After she told us the story she looked as if she'd found something that was lost a long time."

Dee ran her hand along the top of the old dusty bar top. "Lizzy said the nurse mentioned that her grandma died with a smile on her face. We just all get so caught up in our lives that we don't stop to smell the roses. I guess Lizzy's grandma smelled the roses that last moment on her death bed." Dee smiled.

"I think I'm starting to understand," I said, thinking back to that time in our lives when all the pieces fell into place–and apart–at the same time.

"We all did *seem* to go our separate ways. I don't remember the fire, but it sounds familiar. As if I do remember..." As I stepped farther into the room, each step sounded as familiar as the memory.

"I *do* remember. That was when Allen and I started dating again. You found Henry's father, and Lizzy had the twins, left BUCKETS and went off to become a novelist."

"Yep. We were all still very connected, though. Life just got in the way. I believe if the fire hadn't happened, together we might have been able to do something with this house."

Dee walked over to the shelves that stood behind the bar. She picked up a wine glass that had yellowed from years of not being used. She dumped what appeared to be a locket, into her hand.

I nodded. "I get it...We lost *ourselves*. We became mothers and wives as well as business women. I was busy running the hardware store, you with BUCKETS, and Lizzy with her novels."

"We lost ourselves... And we stopped chasing butterflies," Dee said softly. "We stopped evolving. We stopped following our instincts. We stopped dreaming. That's *exactly* what we lost. Don't get me wrong, we still had each other and were connected, but we became adults, with responsibilities, and became a *product* of our lives."

"That's exactly what I meant when I told Lindsey *I wanted to live,*" I said aloud. I glanced behind the old slanted bar top; there stood a transparent female figure.

She stood with her hands folded in front of her. She graciously nodded her head towards me. *Am I really seeing this?*

"I understand...That's why we're here. I needed to chase my butterfly." I looked again at the female figure as she faded away. "I never did... until today..."

Dee smiled and gave me a confirming nod. "My job is done here. Let's get to the garden." Dee made her way to the door and opened it. "You coming?"

I hesitated, still embracing my newfound thought. "Yes, yes the garden." I walked towards the door. "That's *why* she wrote the book...so we would always be together."

***

"Where are we now?" I glanced around the dirt road that twisted and turned, for what looked like miles. Cabbage fields and cow pastures hugged closely to the road as we walked.

"We are Dirt Road Dreaming baby!" Dee laughed. "You know Lizzy and I did a lot of dreaming on these roads."

"You did?"

"Yeah, we did...You know, you were with us."

"I was?" I stopped in my tracks.

"Well, not *physically* with us. Each dream we came up with, you were a part of it." Dee motioned me to keep walking. "Just like right now, Lizzy is with us. We learned a lot riding these roads. Especially about ourselves."

"Me, too." I giggled. "I lost my virginity on a road that looked just like this. It was one of the Harris Brothers."

"Which one?" Dee asked.

Randy Harris, I thought.

"Randy! No way!" Dee shouted, slapping her hand to her knee.

"How did you know?" I asked, feeling my face turn warm. "I didn't say that out loud."

"Remember, we're connected. No secrets here." Dee grinned.

I sighed with the memory. "We were driving around and got a flat tire. We sat for hours talking. He kissed me. Ohhh, I thought he was so darn cute. It just happened. Then he wanted to get married but we were still in high school. I couldn't get married. I didn't even know if

I *liked* him. So after we went back and joined the rest of the world, I completely blew him off. I acted like I didn't know him. I think I broke his heart." I kicked at a stone.

"Wow, why didn't you ever tell us?"

"I felt horrible about treating him that way. I think I convinced myself it never happened."

"Seems you learned a lot out here, too."

"Yes, I did...." I smiled, realizing I was still learning from the dirt roads. I gently rubbed my hand on Dee's shoulder as if to thank her.

"We are here."

Suddenly the dirt road was gone and we were standing on the driveway of Dee's home.

"Let's go check out the garden," she said.

CHAPTER TWENTY

LIZZY'S PICNIC

"Beloved, let us love one another: for love is of God; and every one that loveth is born of God, and knoweth God."-1 John 4:7

2004

Finally, Saturday arrived. Lizzy's excitement sparkled, lighting up her home. Having Dee, Henry, Ripley and Lindsey come for a picnic gave her something to look forward to. She even whistled as she prepared the sandwiches for later. She prepared her fairytale tea and iced it down. *All of us could use some fairy tale in our lives!* A bark from Tank alerted her that someone had arrived. Dee's truck rolled down the long driveway.

"Oh they're here." Lizzy quickly packed the basket and made her way to the front door.

Dee was already out of the truck and looking at the lawn mower. Henry stood holding a bug habitat with a tiny butterfly in it. He was so cute. Every time the butterfly fluttered, Henry talked to it. Tank and Bella sat patiently in front of Henry.

"Hi, Aunt Izzy! My daddy said he might come, too!" Henry announced.

Dee looked up from the mower. "I hope you don't mind. Alo really looked excited when Henry told him about fishing."

"Of course it's okay. I made extra sandwiches." Lizzy winked.

"I'll get started on the pasture so we can visit while they fish," Dee said, turning to Lizzy and rubbing her hands together to get the dirt off.

"So how has it been going? You know, having Alo around?" Lizzy asked.

"It has been good. It has been *really* good." Dee whispered with a sly smile.

The tiny butterfly fluttered excitedly inside the habitat, which caught Lizzy and Dee's attention.

"Mommy, he wants to get out of the cage," Henry announced.

"Go ahead, honey. Set him free." Dee smiled at Lizzy. Henry unlatched the tiny door of the habitat and released the butterfly.

In a bouncy flight, the butterfly hovered around Lizzy's head whispering, twinkling love dust, without a need for sound. She could feel the pleasant flutters brush her face as the butterfly passed, almost as if it had kissed her cheek. *Butterfly kisses.* Lizzy beamed, enchanted by the butterfly.

She watched the butterfly with a lump in her throat. Her heart felt a peacefulness; she stood mesmerized. "What a beautiful butterfly... he was in your garden?"

"We have to make a wish!" Henry shrieked and snapped Lizzy from the magic hold the butterfly had over her.

The three of them each made their wishes. The butterfly circled them three times and fluttered off toward the pasture.

"Okay, I'm going to get the grass mowed. Henry, you help Aunt Lizzy get the fishing poles and picnic stuff together. Henry brought his wagon." Dee strolled to her truck, lifted the wagon from the back and grabbed two small fishing poles.

"You can use this wagon to haul it all to the lake."

"Great idea," Lizzy said, eyeing the wagon. She had not thought of how she would get everything out there.

"Henry's idea!" Dee said, then rubbed Henry's head as a proud mother would.

She went back to the riding mower, put on her giant straw hat and hopped on. She started it up and the engine purred. "Joe got it running good," Dee yelled over the noise of the mower.

"Yes, he spent the whole day on it," Lizzy shouted back. Dee nodded and off she went.

Lizzy felt so blessed for Dee's friendship. Ripley's too, for that matter. Most of the parts for the mower came from the hardware store and Ripley had insisted on giving him a discount. *Gotta love em'!*

"Let's get that wagon loaded, Henry," Lizzy ordered with a smile.

They worked like busy bee's would, carefully placing in the food and then the special tea and quilts. Tank and Bella lazily watched from the porch. They looked like they had given up on the idea that

Henry was going to play with them, until Ripley and Lindsey pulled into the drive.

Tank let out a bark and looked at Lizzy. Bella followed suit. "It's okay, boy. It's just Ripley and Lindsey."

Their tails began to wag with excitement. They too were enjoying the fact that they were having company.

***

Lizzy flapped the quilt into the warm breeze in the pasture beside the lake. It gently floated to the ground. Henry and Lindsey stood by the lake picking out a spot to cast the poles. The warm crisp breeze pushed the smell of fresh cut grass in their direction.

Dee zoomed back and forth on the mower sure to get every blade of grass.

Ripley unpacked the wagon with the iced fairytale tea and sandwiches. The trees swayed in the distant and the leaves of the oak that grew by the lake rustled in the breeze. Today was a perfect day for a picnic. The hot sun beamed onto the lake and rippled the light off the water.

"I just knew you were pregnant with twins. You were just growing too big, too fast," Ripley mentioned again for the fourth time since she had arrived. Ripley sucked the juice from a warm boiled peanut; Lizzy had packed for something to munch on.

"I called Joe to tell him right after the appointment. He has been dying to get home to us. It isn't going to make them get here any quicker, though."

Lizzy plopped down onto the quilt and glanced at Dee on the mower as she zoomed past. "We really appreciate you guys helping us out here. If I get too much bigger I am gonna need help with the rest of the animals, too." Her hand lay on her protruding belly.

"You'll probably be on bed rest the last few months. That's what happened with my cousin Mary when she was pregnant with the twins." Ripley dropped down beside Lizzy.

"I guess... I'll just take it one day at a time." Lizzy smiled as she bit into an apple she had grabbed out of the picnic basket. Ripley leaned back onto her elbows.

Lizzy glanced out at the lake–then gasped. "Oh my God! Where is Henry?" Lindsey stood holding a fishing pole but no Henry. Lizzy struggled to get to her feet.

Ripley jumped to her feet and ran towards the lake. She shrieked to Lindsey, "Where is Henry?!!"

Lindsey turned in a full circle. "He was just here."

Lizzy followed as fast as she could. Panic threatened to choke the breath out of her. *He can't swim very good. I have to check the lake.* Lizzy and Ripley ran to the lake. *No Henry.*

Dee must have noticed the commotion. She headed toward them on the mower. She must have realized they were all searching for Henry. Frantic moments passed as everyone searched for Henry. Dee jumped off the mower, rushed around the lake and scanned the entire property. "Henry!" Dee screamed.

The sound of crumbling brush crunched in the distance and it caught their attention. Through the tall pines that lined the property, a lanky man on a horse trotted up. Henry sat unharmed in front of him in the saddle. It was the neighbor's son, Allen Watson. *Thank god...*

All three of the girls let out a sigh of relief.

"I think this fellah belongs to y'all," Allen said as he dismounted. "He was chasing a butterfly when I found him." Allen grinned. "I was rounding up the cattle when I caught sight of him."

His eyes darted to Ripley and his jaw dropped open. "Ripley Smith!" His grin grew three times in size. "It has been years..." He removed his hat and strode towards her.

Ripley seemed to be just as amazed at the sight of him as he was to her. Ripley gazed up at the tall cowboy. In unison they both said, "You look great!"

Ripley followed with a bashful laugh. Allen smiled and replaced his hat, which shadowed his cheeks that were on the verge of turning red.

"Want to join us? I have some tea and sandwiches. I made plenty." Lizzy offered, still holding her hand on her heart to keep it from pounding out of her chest.

Dee agreed as she helped Henry down from the horse. Standing with her hand on top of Henry's head, she patted it. She bent down to look Henry in the eyes. You could see she was still shaking from the fear. She held both of his shoulders to make sure she had his full attention.

"You can't just run off, Henry. You scared us."

"I sorry, Mommy." He whispered into Dee's ear. From the look on Dee's face it must have justified his actions. She smiled and kissed his forehead. "You scared me to death..."

Lizzy went over and rubbed the top of Henry's head. "Me too, kiddo."

"You just need to say something to someone, honey, so we don't worry." Dee stood and the same butterfly flew past her head.

"There he is..." Henry again chased after the butterfly. In the distance towards the house, Lizzy squinted to see. She noticed a motorcycle entering her long driveway.

"Dee, I think Alo just pulled in."

Dee hopped on the mower and started toward the house. "Henry, you stay where we can see you!" Dee yelled as she pulled away.

"I will, I promise." Henry danced around following the butterfly that seemed content to hover in the pasture where they were set up.

Allen and Ripley stood catching up on old times as Lizzy plopped back down on the quilt. She let out a sigh of relief, again. Henry sure gave her a scare but somehow it all worked out. She watched Henry chase the butterfly as Ripley and Allen rekindled a friendship from the past. Lindsey returned to the pond and cast out her line.

Lizzy turned towards the house. Dee and Alo walked the road that ran beside the pasture. A feeling of completeness came over her. *All I am missing is Joe.*

Lizzy smiled and glanced again at the house and at that very moment, Joe's truck rolled into their driveway. She struggled again to stand.

Dee and Alo walked towards the blanket. Ripley and Allen stood by his horse chatting about high school.

"Oh my...it's Joe. He's here!"

***

Lizzy's nerves finally calmed from the shock of Joe returning home and Henry's disappearance.

Thank God for Allen. All of the emotions storming in her head became tranquil again.

Joe had made it home just in time for the picnic and made her already perfect day, more perfect. How complete everything seemed to be.

Ripley and Allen seemed to be hitting it off. *They always did have some kind of chemistry.* Lindsey and Henry fished peacefully by the lake. Alo and Joe too seemed to have bits of conversation. Alo even offered to help around the property when Joe headed back. Joe seemed content with the idea almost as if his worries had also settled. Dee finished mowing and then relaxed on the quilt still wearing her giant straw hat.

"We should do this more often. It feels good, you know." Dee's voice broke the thoughts bouncing in Lizzy's head. "How long you home for?" Dee blocked the sun from her eyes enough to look in Joe's direction.

Joe got to his feet. "Just for two days." He wiped the sweat from his forehead. "The job we were supposed to start, they delayed, so they let us come home." He looked out to the lake. "I think I'm going to try my hand at some fishing. Alo, you up for some fishing?"

"Sure, my people are *great* fisherman," Alo answered Joe then turned to Dee and winked.

Allen noticed the men headed to the lake. He honestly looked like he was a little nervous to be left alone with so much estrogen in one place. He turned towards the lake. "I think I should probably show these fellows how a real man fishes."

Once he was out of hearing distance Ripley squealed, "Oh my god, he is adorable. I can't believe he still makes my heart flutter."

"He's good with Lindsey, too," Dee said before she sipped her tea and nodded toward the lake.

Lindsey stood holding her pole as Allen untangled her line. He baited it and then patted the top of her head. He was definitely a man that enjoyed children.

"I forgot you guys use to be an item," Lizzy said just before she bit into her egg salad sandwich.

"I can't believe how tall he is now. When we graduated, he was my height. I guess he was a late bloomer. Where did he go off to after graduation? Did he say?" Ripley asked.

"The army. He enlisted right after high school graduation," Lizzy said.

"They sure fed him good." Ripley fell onto the quilt and admired him from a distance.

The three women watched towards the lake as the men battled over a small fish Henry had caught. "It's taking all three of them to get that fish off the hook." Dee laughed.

"Today was really a great day..." Lizzy placed her right hand on Ripley's shoulder and with her left hand patted Dee's leg. *Connection of the constellation.*

"Sure was..." Dee added from behind her straw hat.

"Indeed it was..." Ripley sighed, still admiring Allen.

CHAPTER TWENTY-ONE

DEE'S UNSELFISH DEED

"Love is that condition in which the happiness of another person is essential to your own."–Robert A. Heinlein, "Stranger in a Strange Land"

2004

Dee opened the door to her home and turned on the porch light. She made her way to the lamp and clicked on the living room light. Alo followed behind with Henry in his arms, fast asleep.

"Thank you. Just lay him on his bed," Dee whispered. "He had a full day with no nap. He should sleep good tonight." Dee sat her backpack onto the couch and watched as Alo took Henry to his room. *It is a pleasing sight.*

Alo returned to the living room seconds later. "Well I had better get going." He stood waiting for a response from Dee.

They were Henry's mother and father. That was all they had been throughout the whole week since he'd arrived. Well, except the first night, which was wonderful. Could she be Alo's lover again? There were strings attached this go round–very important strings.

"Would you like a drink?" she finally asked. It was not planned, it just came out. "Tea? Coffee? Or, I have a nice bottle of chardonnay."

"Sure, I would love a glass." He followed Dee into the kitchen. "He's a great kid Dee..."

"Isn't he?" she piped in as she opened the fridge to grab the bottle of wine from the fridge.

She set the bottle on the counter and opened the cabinet. She hesitated for a spilt second. She picked up two wine glasses and turned around. Alo stood directly in front of her, only inches away. Her belly knotted with excitement. "He adores you, too."

She exhaled trying to block out and cover up her utter attraction to him.

Alo moved closer, gripping the glasses she held. He leaned in so close she could feel his sweet breath against her lips. *This is going to be some kiss....*

"Let's go to the garden," she whispered through the moistness of his mouth. "So we don't... wake Henry..."

He lifted her, swinging both of her legs in one arm, and held her back with the other, while gently kissing her bottom lip. She reached for the bottle that sat waiting on the counter with one hand, and still held tightly to the glasses with other hand.

Alo carried Dee out the front door, down the pebbled path, and into the garden.

Oh, he has some powerful hold over me... as if the powerful hold had transformed her from a loving mother into some kind of sexy goddess. Just like the legend of Kokapeli, who enchanted the villagers with his music.

He sat her in the swing. "Let me do the honors."

He opened the bottle of wine as she held the two glasses. He poured each glass, not once taking his eyes off her. He sat the bottle on the ground beside the swing and sat next to Dee.

"To our son!" He raised his glass and Dee raised hers. "And...to us!" he added.

Us? He still believes there is an us! Dee sipped her wine with a smile that stretched from ear to ear.

He placed his lips on hers again. The wine from his lips was much sweeter than the sip from the glass. She placed the glass on the ground to taste more of his lips.

Gently he lifted her onto his lap then he stood. He walked her over to a patch of mint that had grown almost blanketing the ground. He laid her into the mint, without missing a second of the kisses she forced on him. He removed her clothes, not missing an inch of her flesh without tasting her.

After exposing all of Dee's skin, he stopped and stared at her. He looked at her as if she was part of the garden. He removed his shirt and tugged at his pants until they both lay in the garden with nothing on but the wine that caressed each other's lips.

"I...I...I love you..." Alo's breath announced to her skin with each delightful whisper.

***

The cool smell of mint brushed past Dee's nose and she realized she had fallen asleep in the garden. The enchantment of it all had exhausted her. She reached down and felt her bare body, which startled her. She sat up looking for her clothes.

Was I dreaming all of this? She licked her lips to taste for the lingering of the wine. The taste was still there. Her clothes were to the right of the mint patch, next to the gardenias. She glanced at the swing.

Alo sat in the swing, smiling, staring at her. "You were too beautiful to disturb."

Dee stood and began to dress. "What time is it?"

"About midnight." He sipped his wine from the glass he held as if trying to taste the memory of earlier.

"You're welcome to stay," Dee added.

He still hadn't put his shirt back on. His bare chest glowed from the light of the moon. The artwork highlighted the toned biceps as he lifted his glass.

"I would love to, but I need to get my clothes for tomorrow."

"I understand." Dee nodded. She knew if he did stay, neither one of them would get any sleep. "I can't believe I fell asleep."

"I meant what I said, Dee." Alo smiled. "I've fallen in love with you and Henry."

Dee stood silent. Did she hear what he just said? She always pushed people away when she heard those words. She had reason then. Now there was no reason-except fear.

"Can we take this slow?" She asked.

"As slow as you would like." He stood and joined her and then kissed her cheek.

She reached for his shirt, which her clothes covered earlier. She glanced down at the mint patch where they'd made love.

An imprint of a Dee-sized butterfly had flattened the mint leaves. She knew at that very moment, part of her fate meant being with Alo.

***

The memory in the garden played over in her head as she brushed her teeth before getting into bed. The mint flavor from the toothpaste must have triggered the thought.

God how she wanted to tell him she loved him too. She just was not ready to let down those walls. Having the two colored people keep showing up saying, they needed the boy. The fear of Alo trying to take Henry from her. The thousands of thoughts that went through her head today when Henry went missing. She needed to do what was right for Henry and no one else.

"I have got to get some sleep," Dee said to her reflection in the mirror as she spit the last of the toothpaste from her mouth.

She dried her hands on the towel that hung from the old wooden towel ring and flicked off the bathroom light. She walked the dark hall toward her room. She glanced in Henry's room as she passed. He was curled up, snuggled into his pillow with his teddy bear tucked under his arm, just as Alo had left him.

She entered her room and plopped down on her bed. Sleep arrived before she even noticed.

*****

She stood grounded once again, rooted to the muck. Unable move except for the sway of her branches and a slight rustle of her leaves.

In the distance, children were at play. The shadowy figure still stood watching or maybe guarding. The distance made it hard to tell. The light trickled through the forest just enough to confirm the shadowy figure was Alo.

How is he able to come here? Alo-spiritual guide. With moments of watching the children play, she could pick Henry out of the group. She watched him as he played.

Henry often glanced at Alo and smiled. The distance bothered her but Alo somehow soothed the feeling of distance. Behind him, two dark shadowy figures stepped out from the cypress tree where two crows sat perched. There stood the same two colored people she remembered. Dee's leaves rustled and limbs shook with fear. She wanted to yell to warn them but with no mouth, she could only creak, as a tree in the wind would do.

"My dearest Dee..." A voice stepped out from an oak tree. It was Dee's father. "Don't worry for Henry. We are all here to ensure nothing will happen to him."

"Who are those people and what do they want with Henry?" Her trunk creaked as she swayed. Will my father understand me like this? How will she communicate what is worrying her? Her frustration was obvious. The leaves rustled more.

He answered, confirming to Dee that he heard her. "They lost their own child. They want Henry to bring him back... From the dead."

"I know Henry is special. He has our gift, Daddy... But he can't bring someone back from the dead!"

"Dee there is more to the tale of the curse. They were the ones that placed the curse on our family...," he added as he walked around the base of her trunk.

"My Aunt Deidra formulated a drink of herbs to try to help save their child. He could not be saved. They became angry and darkness covered them. The curse was meant for my aunt, only."

He paced around Dee. "She took me in as her own and it changed everything. It brought darkness back into her home. I was a child, the same age as their child was. They wanted to take me from her."

He stopped in his tracks directly in front of Dee. "Our connection and love was too strong, so their darkness still lingers in that house, waiting for the next child to enter. That is the darkness that you and I have seen."

"Oh god, Daddy, Henry and I go there all the time..." Dee's limbs wilted.

"The connection of your constellation is now complete. If you do not destroy the old house, the connections will separate and you will live eternity separated from one another. All of you! It is up to you to rid each of you of a fate without one other. The only way to end the curse is to rid yourself of the house, so Henry never experiences the darkness," Dee's father explained.

"But Daddy I love that house." Her limbs shivered.

"The house holds their spirits, their darkness; you will be helping them, too. It will send them to be with their son and to the light. They will no longer haunt Henry. He will truly know he is gifted and has not been cursed. He will never see that darkness as you and I have..."

***

Dee woke with sweat dripping from her temples. Her heart raced. She sat up and looked around her room. She glanced at the clock realizing it was morning and she had only been dreaming. The dream ran through her head again, everything her father had said to her. She knew what she had to do.

Alo came to take Henry to the beach. Dee had decided he could have alone time with Henry. She felt Alo had already proved himself a hundred times over.

She and Henry were never apart except when she worked at BUCKETS and Dee allowed very few people to watch Henry for her. Lizzy, Ripley and the preschool were the only ones she felt comfortable leaving Henry with. *But, Alo is his father.*

Once Alo arrived, they loaded Dee's truck with the beach chairs and boogie boards. Alo left his motorcycle for Dee in case she needed it.

When Alo and Henry pulled out of the driveway, Dee strapped on the helmet. She knew what she needed to do. Sadness swept over her for a moment. She was not a materialistic person but that old house was not just a possession. She had an attachment to all of the stories her imagination had built over the years.

She could not risk the darkness affecting Henry. She also could not take a chance on the separation of everyone. Her desire to keep the house was not an option. She straddled the motorcycle and kick started it. It roared with just one try. Off she went...

***

Dee crossed over the railroad tracks and stared at the old house, which did not seem as enchanting as it once had. Now it seemed more of a threat. A threat to her new found family and her friendship with Lizzy and Ripley.

Today she struggled to see the greatness it brought to her life but darkness shadowed each memory. Sometimes holding onto the material things we love, can create paralyzing fear. Not losing the people we love the most, because of that fear, is far more important.

The oak stood in the front of the house; two crows perched in the tree, just as her dream had showed her. The oak looked as if it was the only living thing left. Maybe the oak represented the good memories that were still there. After all of the work and painting Dee had done to the house, it still seemed as though it needed fixing.

She stepped on the old wooden porch. The house knew why she was there. The curtains she and Henry had put up last month, had already faded, as if to not look so pretty to Dee. The fresh paint too seemed to be peeling, and even the boards she had replaced were warped. The life that the house once had now rested peacefully in the darkness that blanketed it.

The new outside light that she mounted outside of the wooden door looked aged. Dee reached her hand up inside it and pulled out a key. She unlocked the door and slowly entered.

Gradually she stepped inside. This go round she was unable to hear her steps on the old wooden floors. She grimaced at the thought of what she had to do. Sometimes letting go of material things to keep those most precious to us is a sign of strength and not weakness. The house was always... only a house. The stories, the memories, and the inspiration she would always have.

She walked behind the bar. Dee looked at her reflection in the mirror, a reflection that slowly changed into her aunt Deidra. The reflection pointed Dee towards a box that sat on the shelf.

Dee opened the box and inside the small box was a locket. She opened it and inside was a picture of her aunt Deidra, Lizette and Lizzy's grandmother with the house in the background. Dee grasped it and held it up to her heart. She brought it back down and turned it over. Engraved on the back it read:

The elements of the three

come together will be.

The stars that align

will continue to shine.

Dee placed the locket in the wine glass that sat on the shelf behind the bar. Her reflection smiled back at her and nodded in confirmation. She didn't know why, she wanted to just keep the locket, but something inside her told her it needed to stay with the house.

She opened the drawer underneath the old rusty register. A pack of cigarettes were exactly where she had left them. She picked up the pack and the matches that sat with the pack. She lit herself a cigarette. She had not smoked in months. She took a few drags then grabbed some old liquor bottles and threw them throughout the old house.

She walked to the door and glanced behind her once more. She flicked her cigarette into the house, walked outside, and stood next to the oak tree.

The crows took flight high into the sky. She watched as the old house slowly burned. White star-like snaps floated to the heavens. A vortex of darkness swirled into the smoke from the fire. The house crumbled as Dee watched.

Cleansing... She strapped on helmet, hopped onto the motorcycle and headed home.

CHAPTER TWENTY-TWO

RIPLEY ENTERS THE GARDEN

"The greatest gift of the garden is the restoration of the five senses."-Hanna Rion

2050

I followed Dee down the stone path and into the garden. The colorful display of flowers and insects of all types twinkled about. The combination of different aromas flowed through the air, as if to taste the sweet nectar they carried.

Dee nuzzled her face into the rosemary bush and sniffed the bush. "You know rosemary helps restore seventy percent of memory, just from sniffing it."

I just had to laugh. Not that I didn't believe her, but because Dee had all but lost her memory.

"You better keep sniffing. I mean, Dee, you have been suffering from dementia for a few years now. It just seems ironic for you to mention the rosemary and memory. I don't mean to find it funny, but it is."

"Well Rip, I think you have a point. It would seem funny, I guess. Here take a sniff." Dee smiled.

I bent and smelled the plant. "This garden holds some of the best memories," I said.

If the color green had an aroma, it would smell exactly like that. Fresh, with a hint of earthy essence. I stood with my eyes closed, still inhaling the scent.

As I opened my eyes, a tall transparent figure stood right where the bush had been moments before. It's Allen!

Oh, how I had ached to see him again and there he stood as handsome as the day I had fallen in love with him. Today he was more angelic and surreal. Snaps of light twinkled around him.

"Hi, beautiful," his tall apparition drawled with a smile. "I was waiting to see you again."

"Told you I had a surprise for you," Dee whistled as she walked towards the swing.

"Oh, Allen...I have missed you so." I moved towards the lighted glow.

"Stay!" he said with his hand upright as if to stop me from getting too close to him. "You cannot join me right now. You still have work to do."

"I just need to hold you once more."

A tear rolled from my eye and down my cheek. Nevertheless, I stopped moving forward. "I ache...I dream... I am so torn. I can't bear being without you..."

He nodded as though he understood. "Deep purple. Remember that song?

"When the deep purple falls over sleepy garden walls," Allen began to sing, "and the stars begin to flicker in the sky through the mist of a memory, you wander back to me, breathing my name with a sigh." He smiled tenderly.

I began sobbing. *He is hearing me. He is here. He has always been with me.*

"You're right. I never left, my dear. I listened every night to you. You held my picture and sang that song. I visited too, while you slept. Every memory was me; every thought; I was with you. Even on that old couch."

He winked at me. "I need you to continue your journey. I will be with you and know we will meet again..."

He began to fade into the green glow of the garden. The words, "I love you..." rustled through the leaves of the rosemary bush. An iridescent green butterfly fluttered out of the bush and circled my head. I turned to follow the butterfly's beautiful glowing trail.

At that moment, I glanced at Dee sitting on the swing and next to her sat another beautiful glow of light. This glow was feminine. I stepped closer. *Lizzy!*

"Hi stranger, I'm glad to see you have still been going to church on Sundays." Lizzy smiled. Lizzy knew church was not my thing.

"Lizzy!" I moved toward her then stopped.

"Do you know why you're here, Ripley?" Lizzy asked.

"I suppose...Well no...Not really. I have learned a lot here. Maybe that's why?" I kneeled by the swing, remembering not to get too close to the glow.

"It's up to you to keep the connection going." Lizzy calmly folded hands in her lap.

"Yeah," Dee said on a laugh. "I'm brain dead, so that's a tough call for me," Dee chuckled. "By choice, I might add."

Lizzy's glow smiled at Dee. "You are too much."

"How?" I finally asked her. "How do I keep the connection going? I have been reading the book."

"You need someone of blood to continue the cycle. Just as we did with the story of the tavern owners. Henry with the hardware store..." Lizzy started to explain.

"Yeah, he would make me tell him that story over and over," Dee interrupted. "How your grandfather started it, and then your father took over. He always loved the fact that you were a woman and continued the family business."

"You need to tell the story. Stories help us live, help us to be remembered. Stories provide knowledge to the next generation. Your blood needs that. We need to live on just like the stars," Lizzy said.

"So what Dee said about us being star people is what we are?" I asked.

"We are the light in the heavens. Angels, messengers, shiny ones, and yes, star people," Lizzy said. She turned to Dee and pursed her lips.

"Stories need to be handed down. The others learn from the stories. Our history teaches them not to make the same mistakes as we did. Our stories teach them to embrace themselves just as we learned to do. It shows them how to think for themselves. We need to become the voice in their heads and help them learn that love is the truest connection."

"Is that why you wrote the book?" I asked.

"It *is* why. Everyone has a story in them. We all search for meaning. It is in that story, our *own* story, we find the meaning," Lizzy answered.

"Yeah, I needed you to read me the story. If you hadn't, we would have never have been able to meet here in the garden," Dee said.

"Every story has reason," Lizzy concluded. "Connection and unconditional love is the reason for this story. You read the story and that has caused the start of connection. Follow your instinct and live blissfully." Lizzy started to fade just as Allen had faded into the colors of the garden.

"Wait! I'm still not sure how!" I yelled into the swirl of colors as they spun into nothing.

"*You* are how... The book will lead you..." Whispered the breeze of fragrant flowers.

The garden was as colorful now as it had ever been. Butterflies danced with the bees hovering over the garden below. The chirping of the birds highlighted the enchantment of the beautiful garden.

***

I paced the garden for what could have been an hour, listening to Dee babbling about "the good old days." I tried desperately to absorb everything Lizzy had said to me.

"So what do we do now?" I asked as I stopped pacing directly in front of Dee and the swing.

"We head back to the forest. Where we started from," Dee said. "We have to get back to our vessels. Old people, here we come!"

Dee grinned and stood from the swing. She flexed her shoulders and stretched out her arms.

"What about the book? Where is it if we are in it?" I asked as I started to follow Dee out of the garden.

"My vessel has it. You didn't think I would let you come here without me, did you?" Dee smirked and continued walking.

"I'm confused as hell."

"You should be. You took a nasty fall. Hit your head, too." Dee continued to march towards the forest in the distance.

"I mean... about what I need to do," I muttered.

"You will know when it's time. Rip, it will be like an epiphany. It will be like De'ja'vu. You'll know. Just trust the voices you hear, just as Lizzy did when she published the first book. She followed her instinct. She gave it to you. She knew you would need it someday." Dee maneuvered her way onto the dirt road. "It's like this: trust yourself–your inner voice–and go with the flow."

***

We slowly came upon the mystical forest. Dee stood gesturing me to enter.

"Wait! Here... You're going to need this on your adventures!"

Dee handed the old locket over to me. I slowly entered the forest between the ash tree and the oak. My body became light as the air and I began to float, just as the butterflies had done in the garden. I looked around the forest and the forest began to change.

***

I was back in the nursing home garden, but I was not in my vessel. My vessel was nowhere to be found. I hovered over the nursing home garden and watched the young transparent Dee return to her old vessel. Dee sat calmly with no expression still holding the book, just as she had before. I was nothing but thought—a soul—a floating conscience. *Where is my vessel?* I watched my precious granddaughter Ashley walk towards lifeless Dee.

"Ms. Dee, I need Grammy's book," Ashley said to her. Young Dee's transparent arms rose and handed the book to little Ashley. Old lifeless Dee sat unaffected; younger, transparent Dee glanced at me. I was nothing but a hovering soul. Transparent Dee winked.

I understand now, I thought.

It took a good knock on the noggin I guess, Dee's voice replied.

"Thank you. Grammy will need to finish reading this to me when she wakes."

Ashley held the book and headed towards the parking lot. My thought followed her. An ambulance's lights flashed throughout the parking lot as it pulled away.

~ 159 ~

"Come on honey, we have to get to the hospital. I don't want Grammy to wake without us being there," Lindsey said to Ashley as she closed the hover car door.

My vessel. My thought followed the ambulance.

CHAPTER TWENTY-THREE

LIZZY WRITES

"I have been reminded of your sincere faith, which first lived in your grandmother Lois and in your mother Eunice and, I am persuaded, now lives in you also."-2 Timothy 1:5

2004

Lizzy's morning started with the one cup of coffee as it always did. Her belly had tripled in size.

Gracey had started her chemo and she sure had a lot of fight in her. She still wanted to keep her shifts at BUCKETS.

Of course, Dee and Lizzy both told her to take some time off. She would always have a job when she was ready.

Dee started training two new girls at BUCKETS. The holidays were soon approaching and they needed to hire some help. Things were changing and changing fast.

Ripley and Allen had been hitting it off so well that there was even talk of a commitment. Lizzy's doctor insisted she stop working and start taking things slow. He also mentioned the idea of bed rest coming soon.

Joe steadily worked as much as he could to get the bills caught up so that when the babies arrived he could take some time off. Lizzy almost felt guilty for the fact Joe desperately wanted to be a part of all that was happening with her, so she made sure every moment of the experience was written on paper. Five different notebooks filled with stories from pregnancy to before she met Joe, scattered across her coffee table. She was a writing goddess. It was very therapeutic for her and it did not take a whole lot of energy.

There was a knock at the door. Tank and Bella raced to the door. Lizzy opened it trying to keep the two of them at bay.

"Hey!" There stood Ripley. "I wanted to stop by and see how you're doing."

"Come in." Lizzy gestured for her to enter.

"I'll take care of Wilbur and the chickens for you while I'm here."

"Thank you that would be great. Tell Allen we said thank you. Joe and I really appreciate you guys helping us out."

"What are friends for?" Ripley smiled and sat on the couch. She glanced over at the pile of notebooks on the coffee table.

"Alo stopped by and fixed the gate out front for me, so let Allen know it's all fixed. Joe should be coming home next weekend so he can fix the chicken coop door."

Ripley inclined her head toward the notebooks. "You sure are writing a lot. I thought you were just kidding when you said you wanted to write a book."

"Nope, I was serious." Lizzy smiled gently as she lowered herself onto the couch. "I just sent out my first manuscript on Monday. It's a surprise for you and Dee."

"I can't wait to read it." Ripley crossed her legs. "I had something I wanted to ask you, too...."

"What is it?" Lizzy cocked her head. "Is everything okay?"

Ripley grinned. "Allen asked me to marry him and I want you to be my maid of honor."

"Really? That's wonderful!" Lizzy glanced down at her huge belly then back at Ripley. "Of course I will be your maid of honor. Just like back in fourth grade when we would play Barbie's for hours, remember? How many times did we marry them off?"

Ripley laughed. "*You* married them off. My Barbie was always at work..." Ripley shifted in her seat. "We don't plan to do it until next year so don't worry about..." She glanced down at Lizzy's belly.

"I also wanted to know if we could have the wedding in the pasture by the lake. Kind of like how we were reunited there."

"I think that is a wonderful idea!" Lizzy clapped her hands together and squealed.

"Alo and Dee are doing good, it seems," Ripley mentioned. "He's going to take her and Henry out to Arizona to meet "his people." I'm assuming that's his family?"

"Yep, he's a Hopi American Indian. Both of his parents are descendants of that tribe. It is amazing, isn't it? Dee was always so passionate about American Indian culture."

"Passionate? More like obsessed." Ripley laughed. "Lindsey was doing a report in school on American Indians and Dee pulled out like fifty books on the subject. Even Alo was amazed."

Lizzy struggled to stand up from the couch, smiling at the thought of Dee. "You want something to drink?"

Tank and Bella's eyes followed Lizzy as she crossed the room. "I made some cucumber water. It is really tasty." Lizzy glanced back a Ripley. "I needed to cut back on my sugar and nothing is sugar free these days. I have tea, too. Sweet iced tea, just like the good old days."

"Sure, I'll have a glass of tea." Ripley stood and followed Lizzy to the kitchen.

Lizzy pulled two glasses from the cabinet. She added ice to the glasses; in one, she poured the cucumber water and the other some tea. "You aren't working today?" she asked as she handed Ripley her glass.

"I went in early this morning and got everything I needed to get done. I left Jacob in charge. I realize I need to quit trying to do everyone's job. It's best I stay away a little." Ripley sipped her tea, then smiled.

"My Dad said I'm a control freak. If I want them to do their job right, I need to give them the opportunity to do their job. I had to laugh because he was right." Ripley laughed. "Kind of funny, I can remember my grandfather telling my dad the same thing."

"Daddies always seem to know best." Lizzy sipped her cucumber water.

"How are your mom and dad doing?" Ripley asked.

"They are good. They stopped by Sunday. They bought a travel trailer, and they are going to travel the country. I told them they had better be back before my due date. My mom said they wouldn't miss the arrival of these babies for the world." Lizzy smiled and rubbed her giant belly. "Oh my god...I forgot to tell you!"

"Tell me what?"

"I'm having girls!"

***

Hours after Ripley left, Lizzy started jotting down ideas for the bridal shower she wanted to plan for Ripley. She knew Ripley hated surprises so that was out of the question. Springtime would be perfect and the feasibility of doing it in Dee's garden was exciting. Lizzy went to the phone and decided to call Dee to see what she thought. She dialed the phone.

"BUCKETS, may I help you?" sounded from the other end of the line.

"Dee?" Lizzy asked.

"Yes. Liz, is that you? How ya feeling?"

"I feel as big as a house." She laughed. "Ripley stopped by today. Did she tell you the news?"

"She did...I hope you aren't upset with me," Dee said.

"Upset with you? For what? If anything, you should be upset with me," Lizzy answered. She had wondered how she was going to tell Dee that Ripley wanted her to stand as her maid of honor.

"Liz, Ripley asked if I would stand as her maid of honor..." Dee answered.

The phone was silent for a moment, then Lizzy laughed. "She asked me, too."

"Maybe she couldn't decide so she wants us both to stand with her," Dee replied.

"She did say she wanted it to be just as it was the day she and Allen were reunited."

"You know what that means don't you?" Dee said.

"We have a bridal shower to plan!" the girls yelled in unison.

***

Lizzy stood out on her redwood deck looking out towards the pasture and visualizing Ripley's wedding day. She planned to have the guests, park their cars to the left of the gate entrance and on Allen's family property too, since his father's land butted up against theirs. First, she wanted to make sure Ripley was okay with the idea.

The butterfly Henry had released zoomed past her head. Behind the butterfly-trailed sparkles of light, which mesmerized Lizzy.

"How nice to see you again!" she whispered to the butterfly as is hovered around the potted plants, which hung from the porch. "I love you..." she whispered again.

She thought back to when things were much simpler. The manuscript she had written brought back many fond memories. Somehow, everything had played out in her life so perfectly. Sure, there were hard times. Without the hard times she would have never noticed the wonderful reasons behind them. Today she did. *Nature's balance.*

Tank and Bella played on the lawn at the bottom of the deck. Lizzy plopped down in the old rocker that Joe had gotten from the neighbor's garbage pile.

"I can make this look good as new," he had said the day he lugged it home.

He did what he had promised and it was so nice Lizzy wanted to put it in the nursery. Joe insisted that they buy a new one for the babies' room, so the old rocker stayed out on the deck. She loved to sit outside so it turned out to be the perfect place for it.

The babies' room was coming along nicely. Pink and yellow were the colors she had chosen. She had gotten butterfly decals to place on the walls above each of the girls' cribs. She gave Henry's butterfly credit for that idea. She even ran across butterfly sheets and blankets for the crib.

Her mother and father insisted on helping foot the bill for all of the babies' necessities and there were a lot.

"Two of everything," her momma reminded her often, but always with joy in her voice.

How blessed she felt. Things were getting better. Life is a roller coaster; it has its vicissitudes, only to make the ride memorable and exciting. *Balanced.*

CHAPTER TWENTY-FOUR

DEE IN TRAINING

"My friends have made the story of my life. In a thousand ways they have turned my limitations into beautiful privileges, and enabled me to walk serene and happy in the shadow cast by my deprivation."-Helen Keller

2004

Dee scanned BUCKETS. It sure was not the same not having Lizzy around. An emptiness whispered through the air. She knew Lizzy would probably not return this go round although she did promise to do the bookkeeping and sales tax paper work.

Lizzy was going to make a soup a week for Dee to sell at BUCKETS. Could Dee really blame her for wanting to stay home with the babies when they arrived?

She remembered how overwhelmingly guilty she felt the first time she went back to work after Henry was born. Not having Gracey working anymore meant BUCKETS surely needed Dee more.

Gracey's battle with cancer was beginning to take a toll on her. *Thank God Alo decided to move here to be close to Henry and me.*

"Dee, I don't remember what button the draft beer is." The new girl, Renee, stood staring at the register. She jolted Dee from her thoughts.

Renee was the same age Lizzy and Dee were when they first opened BUCKETS. "Right here." Dee pointed to the correct button. "Make sure you scan the bar for any empty bottles," Dee coached. Things were changing and somehow it all seemed to be okay. *You can't live off old successes, you have to make new ones.*

"Hi, Mommy!" Henry's voice yelled from the front door of BUCKETS. Alo followed looking exhausted. "We went to the park and played," Henry said as he made it to the end of the bar to grab a hug and kiss from his mother. Alo arrived as Dee set Henry back down.

Alo kissed Dee. "We played very hard at the park. He should sleep well tonight." Alo winked at Dee, their secret communication about spending some time together later. It was nice that they were Henry's parents, but they also had some sort of connection besides Henry. Maybe it was love, but more along the lines of something unconditional, than romantic.

"Looks like you should sleep good, too." Dee giggled at Alo's tired face. It sure was nice having him around.

Dee knew things were changing and normally she hated change. Over the years, she came to realize that change was inevitable. This time the change seemed to be more for Henry's sake, the twins, and Lindsey, than their own. That seemed to make it even more needed. Sure, she was scared but she knew Lizzy and Ripley were always only a phone call away. As long as they held a promise to always meet, she was content with the idea of living separated but yet always together.

"Dee, are you okay?" Alo asked. He must have seen the look of distance in Dee's eyes.

"I am...I actually am."

"Ms. Dee? I just got an order for wings. I haven't made those yet." Renee stood by the kitchen doorway looking lost.

Dee made her way to the kitchen. "Well I guess I'll need to show you then. Lizzy was always so much better at training in the kitchen," Dee babbled as she grabbed a pack of frozen wings from the freezer.

One by one, she placed them into the hot oil as Renee watched and learned.

***

Evening began in the garden, after she tucked Henry into bed and fast asleep. Dee and Alo sipped wine from their glasses as they swung in the swing. Dee turned to Alo. She saw that when one seat became empty; someone or something eventually filled that seat. Who better to fill the seat than Henry's father?

"I have been thinking a lot, Dee," Alo said, looking out over the garden. "We should take Henry on a trip. The three of us. Like a family vacation."

Dee smiled, kicking her feet.

"Road trip!" they said in unison.

Dee gave him a quick kiss, thankful he was there to fill her slight feeling of loss. She wasn't even sure what the feeling really was. *Change? Time? Maturity?* It was like sand falling through an hourglass and there was clearly more at the bottom than the top.

Alo grabbed her at the nape of her neck with one hand, and pulled her toward him. Oh, the power he had over her. Dee gave into each seductive kiss. He made her feel she was capable of anything. He was her drug and she wanted more of it.

"Have you ever been sky diving? It's better than sex," Alo whispered. He kissed her neck.

"Always wanted to...I..." Dee honestly could not have conversation right now–he was taking her to her place of euphoria and he had the same sense of adventure as she. "We should..." she began.

"Yes, we should..."

CHAPTER TWENTY-FIVE

RIPLEY AWAKES

"Live a good life, and in the end it is not the years in a life it is the life in the years."-Abraham Lincoln

2050

"Mrs. Watson? Can you hear me?" I hear in the darkness that suddenly turns to a flash of bright foggy lights.

I feel my eyelids lift and hear commotion bubbling around me on what seems to be a magnetic gurney hovering in a forward motion.

Intoxicated by the feeling of life for a moment, I speak. "Where is my Granddaughter?"

"They are on the way," a female voice answers.

"What happened?" I ask.

"You fell and hit your head. Possible concussion. Do you know what day today is?" the foggy male voice asks.

"Today? All I know is... today is my first day of living." I sigh with contentment.

"How old are you?" the female voice asks.

I answer proudly. "Eighty."

"What is your name?" the male voice asks.

Well, for goodness sakes! "Ripley Watson. Shouldn't you *know* all of this?" Aggravation rattles my voice and I really don't care.

"We need to see if the trauma has affected your memory," he explains.

"My memory is fine. Where are my daughter and granddaughter?" I ask, struggling to sit up.

"Right here! Right here!" Lindsey's voice travels to me from a distance. The clicking of heels sounds on the metal floors.

The gurney stops moving and the voice of my daughter moves closer.

"Here we are, Mom. You're conscious... Thank god." I feel my daughter's hand touch mine. "They couldn't wake you..."

"I'm fine. Hit my head, I guess. It hurts like hell." I smile and rub my head in the spot that must have hit the rock. I realize I'm still holding the locket Dee gave me.

"What is that?" Lindsey asks taking the locket from my hand. She opens it. "How nice. It has a picture of you, Ms. Lizzy and Ms. Dee. Wow, you were so young in this picture." I have to smile. *Yes, once upon a time, we were young.*

"How's Dee?" I ask.

"She never moved a muscle. Honestly Mom, she has no idea of what's going on around her." Lindsey says handing the locket back to me. I grasp it tightly and smile again. "Sure she does." I snicker, just like Dee would.

"Grammy, I got your book." Ashley's voice sings from the bubbling of people moving around the gurney.

"Good, sweetie. We're gonna need it," I say over top of the wall of hospital workers.

They roll the gurney into a small private room. The walls that now surround me muffle the noise of the hospital.

"We just need to monitor her for a bit. Run some tests. Just to make sure she's okay," I hear the obscured male voice say to Lindsey.

"This will help you relax," a female voice says just before the stinging sensation pinches my arm.

"Ooh..." I drift off.

***

"Twinkle, twinkle little star, how I wonder what you are... Up above the world so high...Like a diamond in the sky... Twinkle, twinkle... She is awake!" Ashley's voice sings as my eyes flutter a bit. They feel like they are glued shut.

"Hi, Mom. How is your head?" Lindsey's misty figure asks.

"Hurts a little. Sore, slight headache. What are they saying?" I ask.

"Looks good. No concussion, just a little trauma to the skull. They did a full scan and everything looks good. Blood work is good. They want to watch you a little bit more because of your age. They said first thing in the morning you can go home," Lindsey adds.

Yippee! "Ashley dear, come to Grammy and bring the book." I lower my hand from the hospital bed. Little Ashley joins me. She hops onto the bed and snuggles close. She hands me the book.

"What are the bumps called again?" she asks me. We open the book to the marker where we left off. The marker was an old thank note Lizzy had written to me years ago. I remember well what it said:

Thank you for understanding. Keep this one for us to look back on and laugh. I promise I will get you one in print. I love you!

Love, Lizzy

P.S. You never know you might want to learn brail one day!

"The bumps are called Brail, my dear. That's how Grammy is able to read," I answer as my fingers run down the page to the start of a new chapter.

"I want to learn brail," Ashley says. "I want to write a book, too. Just like this story. I love books; I wish they still made them."

"Oh, honey, this is more than a book. They were more than friends. We had a connection. A bond. A special something that some people live a lifetime and never feel. These were some of the best years of my life." I add.

"Lindsey, dear? We should take a trip... New Orleans... I've always wanted to go to the bayou... Niagara falls, ohhh, and Vegas, too."

"Sure, Mom, let's get you well first." By the sound of Lindsey voice, I know she's unsure of what she has just heard me say. *She probably thinks it's just the bump on my head talking. Do I have news for her.*

"And you, Ms. Ashley, Grammy will teach you how to read brail." I tap my granddaughter's nose. I smile and began to read.

CHAPTER TWENTY-SIX

LIZZY'S GIFTS

"Every good and perfect gift is from above, coming down from the Father of the heavenly lights, who does not change like shifting shadows."-James 1:17

2005

After months of preparing for the twin's arrival, today Lizzy and Joe planned to have the birth of their baby girls. Doctor John said that after thirty-seven weeks the babies would be healthy enough to be delivered. They had grown to a very good size.

He suggested cesarean delivery as soon as the thirty-seventh week arrived. For Lizzy, thirty-seven weeks could not have come quick enough. She could hardly walk on her own.

"I have your bag loaded up. We need to be at the hospital by five A.M.," Joe babbled nervously as he shuffled across the room holding a cup of coffee in his hand.

Lizzy just watched from the couch as he paced. She was nothing but one giant belly.

"I could kill you right now for that cup of coffee," she growled. "Why can't I have anything to drink or eat? Could you please explain it to me again?" Her aggravation was apparent. Her feet were swollen and so was everything else.

"Anesthesia. It's so you don't get sick," Joe snapped. He walked to the kitchen and chugged down the last of the coffee. "Let's get you loaded up," he said when he returned.

He helped her to her feet. Tank and Bella watched as if they knew something big was about to happen. A whimper came from Bella, almost a female cry of assurance.

Joe helped Lizzy into Ripley's car. The jeep and the truck were too high to get Lizzy in them. It was a good call on Ripley's part to offer her car. Ripley was going to bring the Jeep as soon as the surgery was over. She had to come see the twins when they arrived. Dee too, was going to meet them there.

"What's wrong with you? You're shaking," Lizzy said to Joe. "How many cups of coffee did you have?" She was moody and she didn't care.

"Two cups! I think I have a right, you know... I'm going to be a daddy!" He hopped into the driver's seat.

Lizzy huffed, "What do you have to be nervous about?"

She thought a minute. She'd never thought about Joe being nervous. He always took things in stride. He never seemed to let things bother him or at least didn't show that things worried him.

Joe laid his hand over Lizzy's and his tone changed. "I am going to be a daddy, today." He smiled that gorgeous smile.

"And I am going to be a mommy," Lizzy whispered.

In that very moment they both smiled and realized everything was about to change.

***

When they arrived at the hospital, Joe pulled the car up to the front door and got out. He looked around for a wheel chair but came up empty.

He held one finger up at Lizzy and mouthed, "I'll be right back."

He shuffled through the doors and returned with a chair on wheels. Lizzy giggled. She noticed how jumpy and nervous he really was. He gestured to the chair with a grin as big as the Milky Way.

He opened the passenger side door and helped Lizzy stand. Joe walked her to the chair and helped her ease into it. He kicked the passenger door closed with his right foot.

"I'll be right back," he whispered, cupping her face and kissing her lips with the pressure of excitement.

He jumped back in the car and zoomed into the parking lot. Lizzy watched, still giggling at him. Moments passed and he returned, still smiling from ear to ear.

"Are you ready?"

"As ready as I'll ever be." Lizzy smiled and he pushed her through the doors of the hospital.

They approached the counter. "We have an appointment for a C-section with Doctor John."

"Name, please?" the receptionist barked in a nasally tone.

"Joe," he answered.

"Sir, are *you* having the cesarean?" She looked over top of her glasses. "The name of the *patient,* please."

Lizzy giggled more. *He really is nervous*.

"Ohhh...Elizabeth Mazzaro." He turned to Lizzy and smiled. "I think I should have had *another* cup of coffee."

"Go on up. They are expecting you." The receptionist clicked away at her keyboard. "Oh wait...I need to put on your bracelets." She stood and wrapped a plastic bracelet around Lizzy's arm. Joe began to push the chair towards the elevator.

"Not so fast, you gotta have one too, Daddy." She wrapped the bracelet around his wrist.

Joe smiled, he was about to be a daddy and if he did not slow down he might miss it. He exhaled the majority of his nervousness and smiled at Lizzy.

"Okay... Go on up," said the receptionist, pointing to the elevator.

***

The doors to the elevator finally opened. Joe twitched the whole ride, Lizzy was sure of it. She could feel the vibration in the chair although he was trying hard to stay calm.

A nurse met them in what appeared to be a designated waiting area. She took them right in through double doors and into a room. She threw some scrubs at Joe.

"Get dressed."

She helped Lizzy get into her gown and onto a gurney. She looked at Lizzy's veins and babbled about her left arm being best.

"Will I be awake?" Lizzy asked. "I would like to be."

"I believe the doctor scheduled a spinal tap," the nurse said as she looked up from her computer. "The anesthesiologist will explain all that to you." Her head turned as a male figure in scrubs entered the room. "Ah! He is here now."

Within the hour, the gurney rolled down a hall and through more double doors. Joe followed not knowing what to do, *but* follow. The room was full of light, bright as the sun on a hot summer day. Only the room was cold and smelled of disinfectant.

"Did my parents say they were coming?" Lizzy mumbled. The medicine must have started to relax her a bit.

"They're on their way," Joe said through the mask.

They transferred Lizzy onto a larger table. They propped her up long enough for the nurse and anesthesiologist to do the spinal tap. Joe looked away as they inserted the giant needle and Lizzy whimpered. They eased her back down onto the table. Moments passed as they prepared her for her procedure.

A nurse placed a curtain just above her chest so she could not watch. Joe sat in a chair beside Lizzy that a nurse had scooted underneath his bottom. He held her hand and sat silently. Lizzy glanced up at Joe. She couldn't move anything but her eyes and head. Groggy from the medicine she asked, "Do you see the babies yet?"

"Not yet. They're still getting you ready for Doctor John," Joe whispered as his eyes followed the organized confusion.

At that very moment Doctor John enter the operating room.

"Are we ready?" he asked looking down at Lizzy. "Let's welcome these girls."

Joe watched and Lizzy glanced at him and noticed his eyes filling with tears. She felt pressure, then the pulling in her tummy became dormant. She glanced at Joe again and saw the tear fall from his eye and at that same second, a baby cry echoed. More pressure and then another cry. Joe's head darted back and forth.

"What do they look like? Are they heathy?" Lizzy asked.

Joe fumbled with his words. His head bobbled as if he was watching a tennis match.

"They're perfect...They are beautiful...They are *our* baby girls..." Another tear fell.

A nurse walked to Joe with a bundle of pink blanket. "Here is baby one, Daddy." She placed the baby in Joe's right arm. He still held Lizzy's hand with his left hand. He squeezed it as the nurse walked away.

Lizzy watched as Joe admired his precious baby girl. Another nurse appeared with another pink bundle but this blanket had white stripes. Joe released Lizzy's hand and accepted the beautiful gift.

"Baby two." He leaned forward so Lizzy could see their beautiful faces. Both girls were content. The echo of another baby cried out.

"Is there another baby?" she asked.

"No, just two," Doctor John answered as he finished working on Lizzy.

Lizzy glanced at Joe. "Did you hear another baby cry?"

He leaned in again to show her both babies were content and perfect.

"Still just as calm as when the nurse handed them to me," Joe said, staring at the two baby girls.

I could have sworn I heard another baby cry...Joey? Lizzy peacefully drifted off into a light sleep.

CHAPTER TWENTY-SEVEN

DEE WAITS

"One day your life will flash before your eyes. Make sure it's worth watching." –Unknown

2005

Dee waited patiently in Lizzy's hospital room while Henry sat at a small table in the corner, coloring. Ripley and Lindsey were on their way.

"Are they here yet?" a voice behind balloons and a large flower planter asked. Lizzy's mother and father.

Joe's parents had already called three times. Everyone beamed with excitement about the girls being born.

Dee felt a lot of excitement and happiness but a hint of sadness also sneaked in. She knew things were changing and knew it was inevitable. She could feel the space that Lizzy and she shared becoming filled with important people and responsibility.

Their whole world and BUCKETS stood as their life for years. Would there be room to add more? Would their friendship be able to hold up through all of the other people and responsibilities?

"Not yet," Dee finally replied with a smile. She cleared her face of any evidence of sadness. Today was a happy day for everyone and her fear was not going to change what was happening.

Ripley and Lindsey followed moments later, each holding a giant teddy bear in their arms. "Any news?" Ripley asked as she sat the teddy bear in the empty chair.

"The nurse came in and said the babies are healthy. Baby One was four pounds one ounce, and Baby Two was four pounds two ounces," Dee announced. "They will be coming in here within the hour." She stood with her hands in her pockets. She thought that by keeping her hands in her pockets, all her crazy emotions would be easier to control.

"You okay?" Ripley asked low enough that Lizzy's parents did not hear.

"Yeah, just nervous I guess...," Dee whispered back. "Just, a lot of memories came to mind." She smiled.

"I guess growing up has made you a little sensitive?" Ripley chuckled.

Within the hour, Lizzy, Joe, Baby One and Baby Two were escorted into the room. The chaos and excitement swirled around the room. Something about babies made everyone think about all the memories of youth, as if, a child being born, made the past live again.

Lizzy's mother told the story of when she had Lizzy. Lizzy's speechless father just smiled, shaking his head, agreeing with her. Lynn, Lizzy's sister, snapped pictures the whole time. She babbled about how they looked so much like her children had looked when they were born. She took two shots of every pose.

"Joe and I decided to name Baby One, Amber Rose. Baby Two is Jessica Sydney." Lizzy was very groggy from the pain medicine, but she still glowed proudly. The baby girls were absolutely beautiful. They had Joe's dark hair and olive complexion, Lizzy's tiny nose and her pretty little perfect lips. They both had curls. Not surprising, because both Joe and Lizzy had curls.

Their eyes looked blue, but just as Dee had remembered, so did Henry's when he was born. The girls were very alert and healthy as could be. Dee heard the doctor saying that sometimes with twins, one might be healthier than the other. That was not the case with these baby girls.

As the chattering of different conversations floated around the room, Dee admired Joe and Lizzy enjoying their first moments of parenthood. Joe looked as though he could not get enough kisses from the cheeks of the babies. Just then, reality slapped Dee in the face and she realized that everything was just as it needed to be.

***

Once the excitement of new babies, wedding plans and her relationship with Alo settled down, Dee recognized a new normal.

Alo talked a lot about "his people" and he wanted Dee to meet them. They had planned to take a trip come summer. Dee straightened the stools at BUCKETS still slightly struggling with the new normal.

The front door opened and the post woman Sandra walked in with a package.

"I have a first class delivery for Dee Bishop?"

"That's me," Dee answered throwing the bar rag in the sink and making her way to the front door.

"Dee? We went to school together. Sandy. We had first period together."

Dee laughed. "Yeah. How are you?"

"Fantastic." Sandra looked around the bar room. "You own this place?"

"Yep." Dee signed the clipboard.

"It's really crazy how we all have grown up..." Sandra took the clipboard back and handed Dee the package. "I didn't think high school was ever going to end. Now I wish I was back there."

Dee laughed. "I know and I hated high school. Really though, I can't say I ever regretted a thing." Dee smiled holding the package up to her chest.

"It was good seeing you." Sandra nodded. "Maybe I'll try coming up some time and have a beer with you. We can catch up on who's who these days."

"I'd like that." Dee nodded back. Sandra vanished out the front door and back to her mail truck.

Dee stared down at the package and noticed a letter attached to it. She slid her finger under the tape that attached it to the package. She opened the letter as she returned behind the bar. The letter read:

Dee,

First off... I so miss you and BUCKETS!

I know you don't find it odd to get a letter from me. Besides, the twins have me so busy I forget who I am. These are the first copies ever printed of my first book.

I had both books encrypted with yours and Ripley's name on them. Please make sure Ripley gets hers. I have no idea when I will get to see her. I already explained to her about the mistake and of course she laughed. Your copy is fine; you know how you always say that things happen for a reason.

It probably won't be until after the girls start day care in the fall that I'll be able to get some free time.

I also wanted to thank you again for understanding my need to be home, and be a mother. And now a published AUTHOR! It is still strange to say that... I do miss being at BUCKETS and I miss all of the customers. Life changes and so do we. I also realize something; I was attached to the friendships that came along with BUCKETS, and I'll always have those whether I work at BUCKETS or not. BUCKETS was your calling. Don't get me wrong, I really enjoyed the ride with you.

Something too I realized: BUCKETS is and always will be part of me and that can never be taken away. It might not have been "me" but it is a part of "me."

I guess in a way I was a lot like a caterpillar eating at the leaves of life,

Oh how well Dee understood what Lizzy was saying. If she had not had to burn the old house down she might have never been able to understand. Houses can be replaced, but memories can never be lost. Everything really does happen for a reason. Sometimes we don't recognize it until years have passed. Dee opened her copy of Lizzy's book and smiled.

"Miss?"

A voice caught Dee's attention. It was a man in a suit standing at the end of the bar holding a brief case.

"Would you happen to know where I could find Deidra Bishop? I have some news about her property at 616 Railroad Blvd. Do you know where I could possibly find her?"

CHAPTER TWENTY-EIGHT

RIPLEY'S ADVENTURES

"A life is like a garden. Perfect moments can be had, but not preserved, except in memory."-Leonard Nimoy

2059

As I reflect on my life, my adventures came later for me than most. I traveled to many places with my daughter and granddaughter, places Allen, Lizzy, Dee, and I always planned to visit.

My poor eyesight doesn't allow me to see the full vision of the places we went, but nothing compares with what the imagination can manifest.

Thanks to the magical book, I ended up reading every book Lizzy wrote to my granddaughter, and before too long she was reading them to me. It turns out, she's a quick study for brail.

I make my visits to see Dee every Wednesday without ever missing one, not ever. My life is complete and filled with all the blissful adventures an old woman like me could ask for.

I carried along, on every trip, the locket and Allen's cowboy hat. Dee, Lizzy, Allen–they were all with me everywhere I went. That was one good thing about not having my vision. I sure must have been some sight talking aloud to the three of them.

Lindsey and Ashley always giggled at me and would sometimes answer for them. My mission? Accomplished, my dear.

Ashley started collecting books because they are obsolete. She has a great fascination with the written word actually coming from a person's original thought and not some computer that analyzed and modified content to its correct format of the craft. That kid is a natural at writing and reading. I am glad I played a part in that.

As for that old house, Dee sold the property off only a few years after the fire. The old oak tree is still there, the only thing left living in the midst of modern mayhem. The oldest natural living tree. The state made it into a National Park.

After Joe died unexpectedly, Lizzy sort of faded away until she too died in her sleep. And that's when Dee's troubles got serious. Yes, it's all about the connections.

When Dee's dementia became apparent to Alo, he became silent. He'd lost her, and he couldn't get her back. It broke his heart, I guess. They were mostly inseparable their whole marriage.

Alo went on a walk to rest beneath that oak tree. He never returned. They say that you can still see the outline of his body in the bark of the tree.

Henry always believed his father went on ahead to help guide his mother to the garden…

CHAPTER TWENTY-NINE

MEETING IN THE GARDEN

"One of the most delightful things about a garden is the anticipation it provides."-W.E. Johns

2061

Halley's Comet passed the earth...

Dearest Dee, I know you can hear me. I made it to the garden. I had to go–Allen and I had a date. That whole Halley's Comet thing, you know?

Lizzy and I will be here when you arrive. I want you to know that it was you, who gave me reason, to continue my work and adventures. I lived and you, my friend, lived with me.

I may have thought I was there for you on those Wednesdays, by reading you the book. It was you who was there for me. Just as we journeyed in the book, we shall journey in the heavens, just like the stars. Finish your work dear friend and we will meet again, in the garden.

***

Dee smiled and closed her eyes. *Finally.*

Many moments passed. Nurse Kathy approached Dee's automated chair that sat in the garden, just like every Wednesday, waiting for Ripley's arrival. Today that was not going to be the case.

"Ms. Deidra? Oh dear, she's cold... Ms. Deidra?"

Although Dee had never really responded to anyone, today was different. Nurse Kathy felt for pulse.

"Oh God. Oh God, no pulse." She quickly called for help.

***

Ten minutes from the nursing home, Henry walked the "nuts and bolts" aisle of the hardware store, taking an inventory for his next delivery on Friday.

The delivery usually came in on Thursday but he asked to have it moved, due to the fact he was going to the service planned for the passing of Ms. Ripley. He always had a connection to her. It was more than just the love of hardware.

Henry was jarred and stopped in his tracks...

My sweet Henry, Mommy has to go now.

The sound of his mother's voice floated above his head.

I love you and know I am always with you. Remember: always use your gift wisely. You are a Bishop and we Bishops have gifts that can better this world. I will be in the garden if you need me, my dear son...

~ 193 ~

A strong scent of roses trailed past Henry's nose. His cell phone began to ring. He knew it would be the nursing home. He wiped the tear that had fallen upon his cheek, reached in his pocket and answered the phone.

Only moments passed and he was in his hover car. He was glad Amber and Jessica, Lizzy's daughters, were still running BUCKETS. His mother would be proud her legacy was living on. Now his mother and father could rest peacefully, together.

He smiled. Of course, the girls had renamed it, TWIN BUCKETS. He thought the idea of two for the price of one was brilliant on their part.

He put the hover car in reverse. As he glanced across the main road of town, he noticed a Grand Opening sign being lifted by two young men and attached to the building.

It was Ripley's daughter and granddaughter's new business venture–in the middle of modern mayhem. The sign above the building read: Grandma's Antique Book Store.

Across the window, a high definition halo-graphic banner read: A blast from the past: Old fashion coffee, tea, and magical books.

***

Dee trudged her way through the forest. She made her way through the sunflower and daisy field. She jumped the railroad tracks. She cast a quick glance at the old house, then smiled as a shadowy figure emerged from the oak and followed her.

Down the dirt road she continued. She moved steadily until she reached the driveway of her old home place. She stepped onto the gravel path that led to the garden. In the swing sat Lizzy and Ripley smiling as Dee entered the garden.

"You're finally here," Ripley and Lizzy said in unison.

"Yep!" Dee smiled. "I had to wait till you guys got here. I never wanted to be in the garden without the two of you. It just seems more magical with you guys!"

She plopped down into the swing, right in the middle of the two of them. She smiled to Alo's shadow in the distance. Things were exactly as they were supposed to be.

~finis~

Twelve Children of the Light and Their Gifts

Western culture

As the brightest ball of light rises in the east, it sprinkled the earth with twelve children of the lights. Each born with a gift. When the brightest ball of light leaves in the west, darkness covers the earth, yet the twelve children of light remained. For the lights would always remain, to remind us that light does exists, even in the darkest hours.

We are all messengers, angels and are born from light to use our gift for the good of humankind. We are the elements that make up our earth, personalities that keep the balance. Differences to make the light complete. Through darkness, we step forward to reveal our appointed gift.

If you were born on the cusp or within days of the cusp, you can have gifts from both constellations. This is due to the placement of the sun at the time of your birth.

Aries (RAM)-(March 20-April 20)-FIRE-Gift of leadership, passion and an inspiration.

Taurus (BULL)-(April 20-May 20)-EARTH-Gift of stability, love, and successful in finances.

Gemini (TWIN)-(May 20-June 20)-AIR-Gift of communication, changeability and intellectual.

Cancer (CRAB)-(June 20-July 20)-WATER-Gift of emotion, adaptability and travelers.

Leo (LION)-(July 20-August 20)-FIRE-Gift of nobility, stability and skills of leadership.

Virgo (VIRGIN)-(August 20-September 20)-EARTH-Gift of cleverness, communicating and intellect.

Libra (SCALES)-(September 20-October 20)-AIR-Gift of reason, analysis and balance.

Scorpio (SCORPION)-(October 20-November 20)-WATER-Gift of secret keeping, steadfast and emotional bearer.

Sagittarius (ARCHER)-(November 20-December 20)-FIRE-Gift of religious expansion, foreign element and learning.

Capricorn (WATER GOAT)-(December 20-January 20)-EARTH-Gift of tangible reality, limitation leader and versatile.

Aquarius (WATER BEARER)-(January 20-February 20)-AIR-Gift of cleverness, stability, and analyzer.

Pisces (FISH)-(February 20-March 20)-WATER-Gift of religious awareness, expandable, and intense emotion.

Twelve Animals of the Light

Eastern culture

Gifted we are, from the time we are born, all living things, each of us a part of the larger light. We are the generations, the cells and the engine of the light. Without us, the *living of the light*, the larger light cannot be. We each play a part in making the light shine.

Your animal of the light is determined by the placement of the moon the year you were born. The moon reminds us that light exists, even in the darkness, just like the stars.

Rat-(1924–1936–1948–1960–1972–1984–1996–2008)-Gifts of creativity, inventions and popularity.

Ox-(1925–1937–1949–1961–1973–1985–1997–2009)-Gifts of brilliant ideas, dependability and great listeners.

Tiger-(1926–1938–1950–1962–1974–1986–1998–2110)-Gifts of courage, bravery, and deep thinkers.

Rabbit-(1927–1939–1951–1963–1975–1987–1999–2011)-Gifts of trust, speaking ability, and a pleasure to be around.

Dragon-(1928–1940–1952–1964–1976–1988–2000–2012)-Gifts of friendship, energy and healthy.

Snake-(1929–1941–1953–1965–1977–1989–2001–2013)-Gifts of luck with finances, and the love of entertainment.

Horse-(1930–1942–1954–1966–1978–1990–2002–2014)-Gifts of compliments, cheerfulness and hard workers.

Goat-(1931–1943–1955–1967–1979–1991–2003–2015)-Gifts of the arts, inquisitive, and full of wisdom.

Monkey-(1932–1944–1956–1968–1980–1992–2004–2016)-Gifts of laughter, problem solving and very good sense of humor.

Rooster-(1933–1945–1957–1969–1981–1993–2005–2017)-Gifts of a variety of talents, deep thinkers and hard workers.

Dog-(1934–1946–1958–1970–1982–1994–2006–2018)-Gifts of loyalty, great secret keepers and concern about everything.

Pig-(1935–1947–1959–1971–1983–1995–2009–2019)-Gifts of honesty, bravery and great students.

FRIENDSHIPS

Jorja DuPont Oliva

© 2015

Friendships are Magical Gardens

manifested on a swing.

Friendships are Mystical Forests

patiently waiting for spring.

Friendships are the Unseen Universe

where the stars are aligned.

Friendships are the constellations

the future may find.

Friendships are the cool fall breeze

that gently will blow.

Friendships are the glistening river rocks

as the waters flow.

Friendships are the twinkling of stars

shining in the night.

Friendships are the perching eagle

preparing to take flight.

Friendships are the musical sounds

of the pounding rain.

Friendships are the comfort and strength

to those in pain.

Because I've written these words

our friendships will never die.

Butterflies are friendships and

now we shall fly.

Our friendship is kindred and always real.

Our Friendship is precious, not even death can steal.

About the Author

Jorja DuPont Oliva is the author of the Chasing Butterflies Series. What started out to be quality time with her mother, taking a "How to Write Your Book in Thirty Days!" class in 2013 by Michael Ray King, has now turned into a three book series. Jorja is a native Floridian and still resides there with her husband and two sons. With the Chasing Butterflies Series now complete, who knows what's in store.

Check out her blog- jorjao2013.com

Twitter: @jorjao2013

lizzyanddeemagicalworld.org

EMAIL: jorjao@msn.com

Chasing Butterflies

FAN Club

P.O. Box 1774

Bunnell, FL 32110